Milo March is a hard-drinking, womanizin[...]
James-Bondian character. He always comes out [...]
combination of personality, bluff, bravado, luck, skill, experience,
and intellect. He is a shrewd judge of human character, a crack
shot, and a deeper character than I have found in most of the other
spy/thriller novels I've read. But, above all, he is a con-man—and
a very good one. It is Milo March himself who makes the series
worth reading.

—Don Miller, *The Mystery Nook* fanzine 12

Steeger Books is proud to reissue twenty-three vintage novels and stories
by M.E. Chaber, whose Milo March Mysteries deliver mile-a-minute action
and breezily readable entertainment for thriller buffs.

Milo is an Insurance Investigator who takes on the tough cases. Organized
crime, grand theft, arson, suspicious disappearances, murders, and millions
and millions of dollars—whatever it is, Milo is just the man for the job. Or
even the only man for it.

During World War II, Milo was assigned to the OSS and later the CIA. Now
in the Army Reserves, with the rank of Major, he is recalled for special jobs
behind the Iron Curtain. As an agent, he chops necks, trusses men like chickens to steal their uniforms, shoots point blank at secret police—yet shows
compassion to an agent from the other side.

Whatever Milo does, he knows how to do it right. When the work is
completed, he returns to his favorite things: women, booze, and good food,
more or less in that order....

THE MILO MARCH MYSTERIES

A Man in the Middle

KENDELL FOSTER CROSSEN
Writing as
M.E. CHABER

With an Afterword by
KENDRA CROSSEN BURROUGHS

STEEGER BOOKS / **2021**

PUBLISHED BY STEEGER BOOKS
Visit steegerbooks.com for more books like this.

PUBLISHING HISTORY

Hardcover
New York: Holt, Rinehart & Winston (A Rinehart Suspense Novel), August 1967.
Toronto: Holt, Rinehart & Winston of Canada, 1967.
Detective Book Club #309, January 1968. (With *Woman on the Roof* by Mignon G. Eberhart and *Who Saw Maggie Brown?* by Kelley Roos.)

Paperback
New York: Paperback Library (63-203), A Milo March Mystery, #2: January 1970. Cover by Robert McGinnis.

ISBN: 978-1-61827-570-7

For Lisa, the girl in the middle—of my heart.

CONTENTS

ONE

There's nothing like a vacation. I was on my second one within a month. The first had started in Los Angeles but had been interrupted by a demand that I do some work.* I did it and found it profitable. Then I collected two very nice checks and took off for Hong Kong without telling anyone where I was going. I thought I was being pretty clever.

My vacation was enhanced by the fact that I was sitting at the pool of the Far Eastern Hotel. There was a dry martini in my hand, a lovely British blonde on my left, and a beautiful Chinese girl on my right. Both wore bikinis. What more could a man require?

In Hong Kong I am often called March *hsien,* which is about the same as "Mr. March." In New York City, where I work as an insurance investigator, I am called Milo March—and sometimes more informal names. I get paid for being called the other names—plus expenses. The last is my piece of the Great Society.**

I had been in Hong Kong for three days and was looking forward to at least two more weeks of no work, no phone

---

* See *The Day It Rained Diamonds* by M.E. Chaber. (All footnotes were added by the editor.)
** "The Great Society" was the name for the poverty programs instituted by President Lyndon B. Johnson in 1964–1965. Apparently Milo would be impoverished were it not for his extravagant fees.

calls, and plenty of whatever I felt like, when there was a rude interruption. From somewhere a loudspeaker squawked into life.

"Mr. Milo March," it said with a very British accent. "Telephone call for Mr. Milo March."

Well, I did know a few people in Hong Kong. I put down the martini, excused myself to the two girls, and went to the nearest phone. I picked up the receiver and said, "Milo March."

"One moment, please," the operator said.

I waited and then heard a voice I recognized. "Milo, boy, how are you?" it said. It belonged to Martin Raymond, a vice-president of Intercontinental Insurance in New York City. I did most of my work for them. I had no idea how he'd found me.

"So sorry," I said in my best Oriental manner, "Mr. March not here. He leave for Singapore. He say he going for a gin sling. Good-bye now." I hung up and went back to the two girls and the martini.

A few minutes later the loudspeaker rasped out my name again. This time I ignored it. The blonde was in the pool and the Chinese girl was talking about a wonderful restaurant where we could have dinner. It was much more interesting than talking to Martin Raymond. I could do without him.

That was what I thought. My name was called three more times within the next hour. I paid no attention. Then the calls stopped and I thought I was home free. I made a date with the Chinese girl and went to my room to get ready. I had a bottle of V.O. in my room, so I had some ice sent up, had a small drink, and then went in to shower and shave.

When I came out, I put on my shorts and made another drink. I lit a cigarette and relaxed while I enjoyed my drink, but I didn't get much time for it. Someone knocked on my door.

I walked over to it. "Who's there?" I asked without opening the door.

"Inspector John Simmons, Her Majesty's Police. I would like to speak with you, Mr. March."

I thought for a minute and then I remembered him. I had been on a case in Hong Kong four or five years before and I had worked with him.* I opened the door and let him in, recognizing him as soon as I saw him.

"Hello, Inspector," I said. "I hope you'll excuse my attire."

"Quite all right, old boy. I should have phoned, but there wasn't much time."

I ignored the implication. "Sit down, Inspector. May I offer you a spot?"

He glanced at his watch. "Perhaps a small one. With water. No ice."

I made a drink and handed it to him, then retreated to my own chair and picked up my glass. "To old memories, Inspector. Cheers."

"Cheers," he repeated. He drank and put his glass down. "It has been some time, hasn't it, Mr. March? The last time you were here it was about jade. What is it this time?"

"A vacation."

His eyebrows went up. "Really? I thought you Americans never took holidays."

---

* See *Jade for a Lady* by M.E. Chaber.

"We do," I said cheerfully. "Why are you here, Inspector?"

He looked at his watch again. "It is true," he said stiffly, "that when you were last here you performed a certain service for us, but in a manner which we found most distasteful. If you will recall, I thanked you for what you had done, but suggested it might be well if you left Hong Kong as speedily as possible."

"I recall. What does that have to do with my present visit?"

He shifted uncomfortably in his chair. "It has been impressed upon me that in certain quarters you may be considered an undesirable alien."

"You mean you want me to leave Hong Kong?"

"Not necessarily."

"Oh," I said. I poured myself another drink. "A bit more, Inspector?"

"No, thank you."

"It seems that we come to the core of the matter," I said. "You want something from me. Is that it, Inspector?"

"I'm only doing my duty, Mr. March."

"I know. I'm only trying to find out what your duty is at the moment. Are you going to tell me, or is it top secret?"

He looked at his watch for the third time, then took a deep breath. "I do not like this any better than you do, Mr. March," he said, "but I've been asked to tell you that within the next ten minutes you will receive a phone call. It is requested that you speak with the man who is calling and consider what he has to say—or you may be asked to leave Hong Kong immediately."

I laughed "Inspector, have they reduced you to being an errand boy?"

His face stiffened. "I think I will have another spot after all, if you don't mind."

I poured another drink for him. "I'm sorry, Inspector. I wasn't laughing at you. I was laughing at someone else. All right. I'll take the phone call. Relax and enjoy your drink. Do you know what this is all about, Inspector?"

"I do not, Mr. March. I received my orders and that was all."

"I think I can guess, but we'll soon find out."

The phone rang. I lit a cigarette before I picked it up. "Yeah," I said.

"Milo, boy," said Martin Raymond, "how are you?"

"I don't know about me, but I can tell you about you," I said. I then went ahead and told him until I ran out of breath.

"That's my boy," he said, "anything for a laugh."

What do you do with a man like that?

"How did you find out where I was?" I asked.

"That was easy, Milo. You had to use your passport and you had to buy a ticket on an airline."

"Now we come to the big question," I said. "I refused to take your earlier calls. Now there is a very uncomfortable policeman sitting across from me who just finished informing me that I should accept this call or I might be expelled as an undesirable alien. How was that arranged?"

"I'm not quite sure," he said. "Happily, I remembered the name of a friend of yours in Washington. He has some private interest in Intercontinental, and I believe he hopes to retire eventually and take a place on our board. I explained the situation to him, and he offered to see what he could do. It was most kind of him."

"Wasn't it? What is the situation and what is on what we laughingly call your mind?"

"Well, we do have a problem and we do need your help."

"You forget that I am on my vacation, the same one I was supposed to be on before, when I was in Los Angeles."

"I know, my boy. I—we—regret interfering, but it is a crisis. You owe us some loyalty, Milo. We are calling on that now. Of course, you will be well paid, including a generous bonus if you break the case."

"You're not just talking," I said. "What's the case?"

"There is a ring operating. We now suspect that it is very well organized on an international basis. There are nationwide thefts here in the States, and there is a general suspicion that a high percentage of the goods are going from here to Hong Kong and then on to Red China. Almost everything involved so far has been insured by Intercontinental."

"Interesting. What are the goods?"

"Almost everything—business machines of all kinds, drugs of all kinds, television and radio sets. As near as we can learn, these things pour into the Los Angeles area from all over the country, then vanish. But we're pretty sure they go to Hong Kong and spread out from there."

"Who are 'we'?"

"Well, we've made preliminary investigations, of course. Then we understand that various local police, as well as the FBI, are thinking along the same lines."

"You say you think it's organized. Do you just happen to mean the Syndicate?"

"Something like that."

"Hundreds of cops are falling on their faces," I said, "and you are calling on good old Milo March to come in as a single linebacker. Is that the picture?"

"I suppose someone could call it that," he said stiffly. "We prefer to think that you're the best man in the business and we wouldn't think of going any other way. You're our boy."

"I thought we outlawed slavery," I said. "Is that your whole case, just as you outlined it?"

"That's pretty much it."

"What about names and petty things like that?"

"I've already put a file in the mail to you. You should have it tomorrow. It will give you the names of the manufacturers of the products, the places where they were stolen, and a fairly complete list of what is involved."

"What about the names of some of the people who have been doing the stealing?"

"No one has yet been arrested, so we're not sure who they are."

"Don't the police or the FBI have some leads at least?"

"If they do, they haven't told us."

"Great," I said, "just great. What makes you think that it's the Syndicate?"

"It's so well organized, it must be."

"That kind of thinking got you made a vice-president? So where am I supposed to start?"

"Hong Kong, naturally. That's why I got in touch with you."

"Do you know that's the place to start?"

"We're reasonably certain that's where most of the stuff is sent."

"It's always nice to start out with a complete file. What if I say no?"

"You'll never get another assignment from Intercontinental. And you might not get one from any other insurance company. Then there is always the question of where you're going to spend your vacation."

"You always were sweet, Martin," I said, "but I was never fully aware that you were merely a heist man in a Madison Avenue suit. I'll take it—but only on my conditions."

"You always do," he said sourly. His voice had tightened. "What are they?"

"First, my regular daily rate—three hundred dollars."

"Agreed."

"You did mention a bonus, didn't you?"

"Of course, Milo boy. You know we have always been generous in the matter of additional recompense."

"Good. I want a guaranteed bonus of twenty thousand dollars whether I solve the case or not. You send me an agreement stating that, and five thousand dollars expense money. When I receive it, I'll go to work."

"What?" he exclaimed. "Twenty thousand! You must be out of your mind!"

"No. I'm in Hong Kong. How much insurance is involved up to the moment?"

"That has nothing to do with it."

"How much, Martin?"

"Fifteen million," he said weakly.

"So?"

"And five thousand in expense money! What do you need

that for? You have plenty of money. We just gave you a large bonus before you left Los Angeles."

"That's fun money. Now we're talking business."

"I never heard of such a thing! Three hundred dollars a day plus a guarantee of twenty thousand dollars plus five thousand for expenses! Why, Sam Spade worked for twenty dollars a day!"

"The price of martinis has gone up since Sam Spade was active. Take it or leave it, Martin. If you don't like it, fire me and get another boy."

There was a long silence.

"Martin," I said, "did you faint?"

He sighed heavily. "All right, Milo," he said. "I'll send you the agreement and the expense money. Will you go to work?"

"As soon as I get the agreement and the money. Good night, Martin. Pleasant dreams." I put the phone down.

Then I picked up the bottle and walked over to the Inspector. I splashed whiskey into his glass.

"I mustn't," he said. "I'm still on duty, you know."

"So am I, Inspector," I said. "I also owe you an apology. I have a pretty good idea of the pressures that were applied to make you come here to see me. What can mere mortals do against the might of Her Majesty's government and the United States of America when they are united? They put on a jolly good show."

"I think I will take another drink at that," he said. "Bailey is on duty and he's a good chap."

"That's the ticket, Inspector."

He stared at me. "I did not mean to listen to your conversation, March, but I couldn't help overhearing something about three hundred dollars a day and twenty thousand dollars. I presume you were speaking about American dollars and not Hong Kong dollars?"

"Right. With all your experience in police work, Inspector, you must be familiar with blackmail?"

"Quite."

"You have just heard me blackmailed into taking a job I don't want. So, in return, I blackmailed them into paying me something that will hurt them even though they can afford it and they expect me to save them several million dollars. It seems a fair exchange to me."

"Quite," he said again, "but astounding."

He'd finished his drink, so I walked over and poured another for him. This time he didn't protest.

"Inspector," I said, "do you know anything about business machines and drugs coming through Hong Kong on their way to Red China?"

"No," he said promptly. "I know the rumors about such activities, but I have no official confirmation. We have investigated, but have not come up with anything concrete. We are aware, you understand, that there is considerable traffic between here and the mainland, yet it is not an easy thing to pin down. We try, but we simply do not have the manpower."

"What about these rumors? Are there any specific people involved that you know about?"

"No names. We have heard that there are Americans and Chinese involved; still we have not been able to get any names—not that we haven't tried, old boy."

"I'm sure you have," I said. "Can we agree on a policy of cooperation?"

"Within reason, my good chap."

He finished his drink. I tried to get him to have another. He adamantly refused. He must have been swacked, yet he stood up with great dignity, said good night, and marched out.

I finished my drink and got dressed. I was debating whether I should have another drink or not when there was a knock on the door. I went over and opened it. There was a Chinese standing there. Not just any Chinese. He must have been close to seven feet tall, and it was all muscle.

"March *hsien?*" he asked.

"Yes," I admitted.

"You are to come with me," he said.

"I don't think you're my type," I told him. "Where am I to come with you? And why?"

He smiled—or something close to that. "To where I take you. My orders are to be polite to you if you agree to come— to bring you whether you are polite or not."

"And if I don't want to come?"

He showed me his teeth again—and then a large-sized pistol. "Then this will be necessary, March *hsien.*"

TWO

He was convincing—or the gun was. There was something familiar about him, but I couldn't quite place him. It didn't seem there was much time for figuring that out. I had a gun hidden away in my suitcase. Even Doc Holliday would have had trouble making a fast draw from there.

"Let's go," I said, "but make it fast. I've got a date a little later."

He put the gun back in his pocket, motioning me to go ahead of him, but he kept his hand in the pocket. We went downstairs and out through the lobby. We marched along the street until we reached a parked Renault. There was another Chinese sitting behind the steering wheel. The big Chinese and I got in the back and we drove off.

We followed a winding road up into the hills above Hong Kong and finally pulled in beside an expensive home. Then I knew where I was. It was the home of Po Hing, a very successful Hong Kong gangster. I had met him several times when I was in Hong Kong before.*

We went into the house and the big Chinese ushered me into a large room. Po Hing was seated behind a beautiful teakwood desk. He was as fat as when I'd last seen him. He wore a silk suit, was smoking an American cigarette, and had a martini in front of him.

---

* In *Jade for a Lady.*

"My good friend Milo," he said, getting to his feet. "I am honored to see you after so many years."

I shook hands with him. "If you're so honored, Hing, why didn't you pick up the phone and invite me, instead of sending your strong-arm boy? Someday you're going to lose a boy that way."

He laughed. "You're the only one I know who might be able to do it. That would be an interesting fight. I shall tell him to be careful with you."

"Just try using the telephone instead of sending him. It's one of those new inventions which may just last."

"Clever, these Occidentals," he said. "I heard you were in town. Looking for more jade?"

"I came on a vacation," I said. "Why the sudden interest in me?"

"You're my friend," he said. "Help yourself to a drink." He waited while I went over to his small bar and poured myself a drink. "I like to be sure you are all right. I still owe you a favor. How are things in San Francisco?"

"I haven't been there in some time. I was in Los Angeles just before coming here, but I didn't get up north. How are things with you, Hing?"

He waved one hand. "Ships still come into the Hong Kong harbor, and as long as they do, Po Hing makes a living."

"I'll bet," I said. "How did you know I was in Hong Kong?"

"There is little that goes on here that Po Hing does not know. I was aware that you were here within the hour after you checked into the hotel, but I waited until you had time to get settled. Then I thought it would be nice to say hello to an old friend and to find out if I could be of any service."

"Maybe you can," I said.

"Oh-ho. Then it is not merely a vacation?"

"It was, but I just had a phone call that has changed things slightly. You have not enlarged your business interests, have you, Hing? I mean beyond the waterfront?"

"No. I make a humble living at what I know best and am content. One of my ancestors, I think, said that it is ambition that leads the tiger into the pit. Why do you ask?"

"Do you know anything about business machines, TV sets, and drugs coming into Hong Kong from the United States and then going on to the mainland?"

"I have heard rumors of such things," he said, "but I have not paid too much attention, since it does not interfere with my business."

"Do you know who is involved in it?"

"No. It is important to you?"

"Yes."

"Then I will find out. I owe you a favor, as I said. I will have the information for you by tomorrow night."

"I appreciate it," I told him. "Only don't send your boy with orders to bring me back or else. Just pick up your nearest telephone and I'll come running."

"I get you, kid," he said. "Have another drink."

"No, thanks," I replied. "The next time. I have a date tonight, and I don't want to keep her waiting."

"Oh, yes," he said with a smile, "you were enjoying yourself at the pool with two lovely young ladies. One was a British girl named Mary Lansing. She is employed at the Hong

Kong Bank. The other was a local girl named Jia Tang. She is secretary to the head of one of our largest export houses. It would be interesting to speculate which one you are seeing tonight. I would guess it is Jia."

"Remind me never to gamble with you."

"I told you I know everything in Hong Kong. What I don't know, I can find out. I will get in touch with you."

"Thanks, Hing," I said.

I left the room and found the big Chinese waiting for me. He escorted me back to the hotel without a word.

It was still too early for my date, so I went into the bar and ordered a martini. I sipped it slowly and thought about my case. Hell, there wasn't any case. There was only a story, and it didn't have a beginning. Raymond had said that neither the police nor the FBI had any names. That was pretty unusual. Normally I could get some leads from the police.

Finally, I said to hell with it and went to pick up Jia Tang. We went to a restaurant she had suggested, then to a nightclub where we danced for a few hours before I took her home. I got back to the hotel about two in the morning and went straight to sleep.

The next day was quiet—no mail and no phone calls.

I spent most of the afternoon at the pool. Finally, about teatime, I went back to my room. I had a quick shower and made myself a drink. If it hadn't been for the call from Martin Raymond, it would have been a fine vacation. I'd always liked Hong Kong. I'd still try to crowd as much relaxation into it as I could.

There was one phone call I'd wanted to make since I'd

arrived. I wasn't quite sure why I had hesitated. The last case here had been one involving stolen jade. I had met a very wealthy Chinese who collected jade. He had made his wealth as a river pirate. I also met his daughter. Her name was Mei Hsu. She was one of the most beautiful women I've ever seen. We'd had some pretty good times together.

I guess I hadn't called her because I knew how difficult it is to turn back the clock or the calendar. But I kept remembering her, so now I made up my mind. When I was here before, she had kept an apartment of her own, although she spent most of her time in her father's house. I still had the phone number of the apartment. I called it, only to be told that the number was no longer in existence. I looked up her father's number and called it. A man answered.

"I would like to speak to the daughter of Hsu Chin Kwang," I said in Chinese.

"Who wishes to speak to the flower of the House of Hsu?" he asked in the same language.

"I am called Milo March."

"Wait," he said.

I could hear a babble of Chinese in the background, but it wasn't clear enough for me to know what was being said. I held the phone and waited.

"Milo," Mei Hsu exclaimed a moment later, "is it really you?"

"I think so. How are you, Mei?"

"Wonderful—now. I was sure I'd never hear from you again. Now here you are."

"How's your father?"

"He's dead. Or, as he would probably have said, he went to join his honorable ancestors, two years ago. I am now the head of the House of Hsu, which undoubtedly causes considerable unrest among those same ancestors."

"I'm sorry to hear about your father," I said. "How would the head of the House of Hsu like to have dinner with the head of the House of March?"

"Love it. Pick me up at eight. Do you remember where the house is?"

"I remember and I'll be there." I hung up, feeling pleased that I had called her. I made myself another drink, then phoned the desk and asked them to have a rental car arranged for me for the evening.

I was just about to get dressed when my phone rang. I picked up the receiver and said hello.

"March *hsien,* this is the one who came to get you last night," he said in Chinese. "You know who I am?"

"*Shih.*"

"There is information for you, but it is suggested that you do not travel in a taxi. The drivers of such vehicles are known to talk like old women. If you leave your hotel and walk two blocks to the right, you will find a car parked. It is not thought that you have to be careful, because it is doubtful anyone is that interested in you at the moment, but there will be no one to remark that the foreign devil went to see a certain person."

"All right," I said, "I'll be there soon."

There would be plenty of time to dress for my appointment later, so I put on slacks and a sport coat. It took me only a few minutes, then I went downstairs. I strolled through the lobby and out to the street. I shook my head at the doorman, who was ready to get me a taxi, and looked around like a man trying to decide where to take a walk. Finally I turned to the right and walked slowly along, looking in the windows. I could see the parked car ahead of me. Before I reached it, I looked back. No one was paying any attention to me.

A minute later I was inside the car, sitting next to the big Chinese. Again we rode up into the hills, and the big Chinese escorted me to the door. I went inside to find Po Hing once more seated behind his desk. I wondered if he ever moved from there.

"Greetings," Hing said. "I trust that this visit was arranged more to your liking this time?"

"It was. But I always feel that I'm riding with a sinister basketball player."

He laughed. "You know, there are a lot of things I miss about San Francisco. Among them are basketball, football, and the Giants."

"Why don't you go back?"

"The fuzz would take a dim view of my appearance. There's a pitcher of martinis on the bar. Help yourself and sit down."

I obeyed him. "Tell me something, Hing. You've told me that you are one of the most successful harbor pirates in Hong Kong. Others, including the police, have told me the same thing. Yet I never see you anywhere except sitting behind that desk swizzling booze. How do you manage it?"

"Sheer brilliance," he said. "I'm the executive type, and I have an excellent organization. I'm getting too old and fat to jump over the sides of ships and then run from the cops.

Besides, I always have an alibi. I'm here getting pleasantly sloshed."

"Clever, these Chinese," I murmured. "Is that why I'm here now?"

"It might come in handy. But I also have news for you."

"I was hoping you might. What gives?"

"It's more than a rumor," he said. "There is a steady supply of business and entertainment machines into Hong Kong from the United States—and of certain drugs.

These are mostly medical, such as antibiotics. I'm afraid that poor old Po Hing slipped up."

"What do you mean?"

"I told you that I'd heard the rumor, but I didn't think it was much more than that because none of those things showed up on any of the ships in the harbor. It never occurred to me that my fellow tradesmen would be so sneaky as to bring the machines in by air freight. I consider it clearly a case of lack of ethics." He smiled as he said it.

"What about the drugs?"

"Brought in by a courier who travels back and forth. He is listed as a salesman for a drug company in Los Angeles, but it is doubtful that he knows anything about drugs beyond heroin. It is fairly well known, although not necessarily to the police, that he brings in more drugs than he displays to the proper authorities."

"How?"

He shrugged. "I would guess that there are hollow bottoms or sides in his sample cases. There might also be a matter of payments in the proper quarters."

"Who?"

"There are five men here in Hong Kong. All of them are tough cookies. Two are local boys. They are Shan Chin and Ma Chok. Both of them once worked for me before they went into business for themselves. Both are killers, but have never been caught. Both are said to have good connections on the mainland. Then there are three Americans. All of them are hoods. Two of them are Larry Blake and Bernie Henderson. They came here two years ago, and as far as I know have never left since then. Blake owns a curio shop in the Wan Tsai District. It's a front, and I doubt if he breaks even. Henderson owns a men's clothing shop not far from your hotel. Good clothes, but I doubt if he makes any money at it—or even tries. The third is the courier, Manny Keller."

"Know anything else about them?"

"Nothing important. Neither one goes near his business, and both carry guns—legally."

"How was this managed?"

He smiled. "Both businesses were held up shortly after being acquired by the Americans. Even this would not be enough in Hong Kong, but I would guess that somewhere along the line they made important friends."

"Do you know what their roles are in this setup?"

"I'd say they run it. Their attitude toward the two Chinese and the other American is that of employers toward employees. I imagine they set the prices, collect the money, and distribute it, as well as seeing that nothing happens to the merchandise between its arrival here and its delivery."

"And the loot that goes back to America is taken by the courier?"

"I imagine."

"What about the courier?"

"Manny Keller? Another tough cookie. He also sometimes carries a gun, but I do not think he has the legal right."

"Does he do anything besides carry things?"

"I do not think so."

"Does he come and go on regular schedules?"

"I am told that his arrivals vary. Sometimes there will be two weeks between trips, sometimes three or four. But my men say that he never stays longer than three days before he goes back to the States."

"Know anything about the air freight outfit?"

"Only that it's a private company. Naples Air Express. I do not know where it originates from."

"Well," I said, "I'm not sure exactly what I have now, but it's a hell of a lot more than I did before. I don't know how to thank you, Hing."

He waved his hand. "You don't have to, pal. I told you I owed you a favor. Besides, I don't like all this new competition coming into town. Have another martini."

"No, thanks," I said. I stood up. "I have another heavy date tonight. By the way, I hear that old Hsu Chin Kwang died."

"Yes. Two years ago. I remember that you found his daughter attractive when you were here before. The rumors are that she is following in her father's illustrious footsteps."

I was startled, for I remembered how her father had built his fortune. "You mean piracy?"

He nodded. "The Dragon Lady of Hong Kong."

THREE

That stopped me in my tracks. It didn't fit Mei Hsu as I remembered her. She was well educated, sensitive, and all woman. With her father dead, she must also be very rich. It didn't make sense.

"Do you mean," I asked, "that you think she is mixed up in this deal we've been talking about?"

"Oh, no. You might say that she practices piracy for charity. I am told that she has a large organization which is busy stealing things from the mainland. I understand that she deals mostly in rare historical objects. She either gives these to societies which are trying to save Chinese culture, or sells them and gives the money to refugees from the mainland." He sighed heavily. "Sometimes I think I should retire. There are too many amateurs in the business."

"Heaven forbid," I said. "Well, thanks, Hing. I'll keep in touch."

"Do that," he said. "You brighten up my days."

I went out and was driven back to a spot near the hotel. I went up to my room. I still had a bottle of V.O., but I called room service and had them send up a martini. I sipped it and wondered what the hell to do next. Thanks to Po Hing, I did have some names, but I knew I needed more than that—not to mention some method of attacking the case.

Finally I filed it away for future thought. I got dressed and went downstairs. There was a rented Jaguar waiting for me. I drove up into the hills. I still remembered the way as well as if it had been only the day before that I had last driven there. It was just eight o'clock when I parked near the big house perched on a terrace overlooking the city. The door was opened by a young man who was obviously a servant. "March *hsien?*" he asked.

"*Shih.*"

"This way," he said in Chinese.

He led the way to a room I remembered being taken to on my first visit. He opened the door to let me in, and then disappeared.

She was standing there waiting for me, looking as beautiful as when I had last seen her. "Hello, Milo," she said softly.

"Hello, Mei," I said.

Then she was suddenly in my arms. I held her tight, and it was as if no time at all had passed.

"I have been feeling as shy as if it were our first date," she told me. "Isn't that silly?"

"Not too much. I put off calling you because I thought you may have gotten married or might be just as happy never to hear from me again."

"Now you're the one who's silly. I'll get a wrap and we'll go."

"Aberdeen?" I asked, when we were finally in the car.

"That would be nice. It was where we went on our first date."

I drove down Bonham Road until we reached Pokfulam

Road. It was a winding avenue that led across the width of the island. We began to leave the hills, driving past the squatter settlements, and finally came to Aberdeen. We kept on going until we reached the waterfront. I parked the car and we walked to the edge of the water, where there were a number of small boats. Several old women clustered around us, all of them talking at once. I chose one of them, and we climbed into her small sampan.

We were soon beside a large boat lit with hurricane lamps. It was one of several floating restaurants moored off the shore of Aberdeen. We went aboard and were met by a man who recognized Mei. He led us to a good table. A waiter appeared as soon as we had sat down.

"Lor Mai Tsao," I told him, naming a Chinese whiskey.

He brought the bottle and two glasses. We had several drinks, talking aimlessly, as old friends will. Then we got up and walked over to the railing of the ship. Below us there were huge tanks filled with live fish and shellfish. There was also a man in a small boat who would net whatever the customer indicated and throw it up on a platform, where it was taken by a cook's helper. Without consulting Mei, I chose giant shrimp, two large lobsters, and a pomfret. Then we went back to the table to have a couple more drinks while the food was prepared.

"You remembered," she exclaimed when we were at the table. "That is what we had the night of our first dinner."

"How could I forget? The food was wonderful, and the company was even better."

She reached over and held my hand for a few seconds.

After dinner we drove into the city and went to the night-club in the Hong Kong Hotel. We stayed only about an hour and then I took her home.

It was daylight when I got back to the hotel. I showered and shaved and ordered some breakfast. I began to feel that I was ready for the new day. The waiter who had brought my breakfast also brought me some mail. There was the so-called report on the case. It gave the names of the companies that had been robbed and their locations. There were also the names of two men who had been arrested with a truckload of stolen machines, but they had obviously been unimportant and had contributed no information.

There was also the bonus agreement and a draft on the Hong Kong Bank for five thousand American dollars. I went and cashed it right away. The money was very pretty. I put it in my pocket and went back to my hotel. I walked into the bar and invested a small part of the money in a martini.

Well, I was on a case. Or was I? I didn't doubt that there were millions of dollars involved, as the report said. I didn't doubt that organized crime was involved; it had to be on that scale of operation. But where did I start? Sure, I had five names—which was more than the home office had—but I didn't have any illusions about how important they were. Two of them, maybe more, were probably fairly important, but only in terms of their own activities. I doubted if they knew anything beyond what they themselves did.

The courier, Manny Keller, must have some contact with others in the gang, but probably didn't know too much either. Discounting the names, I had to think of someplace to start.

Obviously, it had to be in Hong Kong or in Los Angeles. Finally, I went to the public phone in the lobby. I called Po Hing.

"I have a car," I said, when I got him on the phone. "May I come up and see you for a minute?"

"Sure, pal. I know that you're partly fuzz, but you give me more kicks than I have had since I used to go to the hungry i in San Francisco. Come on up."

I drove up to his house. The big Chinese opened the door and led me to the private study. Po Hing was still behind the desk. He waved as I came in.

"Want a drink, pal?" he asked.

"Not at the moment," I said. "If I want a new passport— but a good one—could you get me one here in Hong Kong?"

"American?"

"Yes."

"The best," he said. "A work of art. Expensive, but you could not find better work anywhere."

"How long would it take?"

"If you're in a hurry, six hours. But then it would cost double. And it must be paid for in American dollars."

"All right. I want one sometime today."

"I will need your present passport. Your picture on it will be copied. What name do you want it in?"

"John Milo."

"All right. You can have it later today."

I handed over my passport.

"Do I guess rightly that you are going to leave Hong Kong and then come back later as this John Milo?"

"I think so," I said. "I'm going to leave. Depending on what happens, I may come right back."

"Then one word, my friend. If you do come back, stay away from the places where you have usually been seen. I suggest a small hotel in the Wan Tsai District. It is called the Tien Hou. I own it. It is not too far from a nightclub called Kai Shing's, which you may remember and which I also own. If you want to get in touch with me, you may do so through either place."

"Thanks, Hing. One more thing. This Manny Keller you told me about—do you know the name of the drug company he works for?"

He nodded. "It is called Five Brothers Drug Company, and it is somewhere in Los Angeles. Is that where you will be going?"

"I don't think so. I don't want to show myself around there just yet. I'll probably go to San Francisco and try to get whatever research I want from them."

"Good," he said. "You may need help when you are there. I have a cousin, Herman Po, who runs a restaurant there. But he has other connections which you might find valuable. If you need him, go and give him this." He handed me a small wooden ball. I noticed that there was a tiny Chinese character cut into it. "He will know you come from me. I will have your two passports delivered to you at the hotel this afternoon. Good luck, pal."

I drove back to the hotel. I stopped at the desk and had them make a reservation for me on a plane for Los Angeles the following morning. Then I went into the bar and stayed there until lunchtime, nursing martinis. I had lunch in the hotel. Later I used a public phone to call Mei Hsu.

"Good morning, Mei," I said, "or should I say good afternoon? How are you today?"

"I feel wonderful," she said. "It must be because you're back in town."

"I hope so," I said. "Mei, I want to see you tonight even if it's only for a few minutes. But I don't want to go on the town. May I come up and talk to you for a short time?"

"You sound so serious, Milo. There are reasons why I should be at home tonight. If you don't want to have dinner out, why not come and eat with me here?"

"That sounds fine."

"Come about eight, then. We'll have plenty of time to talk—if that's what you want."

"All right. If I'm delayed for any reason, I'll call you."

I stopped in the lobby and bought a newspaper and a couple of magazines, then went on up to my room. I called room service and had some ice brought up. I took off my shoes, coat, and tie, poured some V.O. over ice, and made myself comfortable. I fell asleep halfway through the first magazine.

It was four o'clock when I awakened. I felt a little better, and I suspected it was because I had decided to do something. I wasn't sure what, but just the thought of not sitting around waiting made me feel good. There was still some ice in the bucket, so I made myself a drink and lit a cigarette. Maybe I could dig up some information back in the States, and then either work from that end or return to Hong Kong.

There was a knock at the door. I went over and opened it.

The big Chinese stood there. He gave me a toothy smile and handed me a manila envelope. I smiled back. I was beginning to feel that he and I were practically buddies. I gave him the money for Po Hing.

I went back to my drink and opened the envelope. It contained two passports. One said that I was Milo March; the other said I was John Milo. Otherwise, they were identical. I put the real one in my pocket and the other one in my luggage.

After finishing the two magazines, I showered and shaved and got ready to see Mei. I drove the Jaguar back up into the hills. The same houseboy answered the door, but this time he had me follow him up the stairs to the second floor. I had never been there before.

He knocked on a door.

"What is it?" Mei called in Chinese.

"March *hsien*," the houseboy said.

"Come in, Milo," she replied.

The houseboy bowed and left. I opened the door and entered. It was like stepping into a different house. It was a large room decorated in modern Chinese with a lot of bright colors. Mei was waiting for me in the middle of the room. She was wearing a red and white Chinese gown with a slit skirt.

"Does it look familiar?" she asked, waving at the room.

"Yes," I said. "It looks like the apartment you had down in the city."

She nodded. "After my father's death, I left the rest of the house as he had wanted it, but I fixed myself an apartment up here where I spend most of my time." She smiled at me.

"You've seen the bedroom, but you haven't seen this part of it. Would you like to mix the martinis for us?"

There was an attractive little bar against one wall. I walked over and made a pitcher of martinis. I carried it and two glasses to where she sat.

"To the most beautiful woman I know," I said.

She grimaced. "I was going to propose a toast to your being back in town. Chinese ladies aren't supposed to do such things; it must be the influence of Smith College. What did—" She was interrupted by the phone ringing softly. She got up and went to it.

She listened for a minute, then started speaking swiftly. But she wasn't using either Cantonese or Mandarin. What was more amazing was that she sounded like a business executive and not the soft, feminine woman I knew. Finally she finished and put the receiver down.

"I'm sorry, Milo," she said, as she came back. "I told you that I had to be here. That was the reason, and I may get another call or two. I hope you will forgive me."

"Inscrutable, these Chinese," I said to no one in particular. "The lady knows that I speak Cantonese and Mandarin, so she switches to a dialect she feels certain I won't understand. No wonder we put up with chop suey when we go to a Chinese restaurant!"

She laughed. "There are many Chinese who speak only a dialect."

"Sure, darling. You answered the phone in Mandarin. The other person spoke, and you glanced briefly at me and switched to a dialect. Shall the scrutable Occidental tell you what the latest word is?"

"What do you mean, Milo?"

I lit a cigarette and took another sip of the martini. "I am told that the daughter of Hsu Chin Kwang is following in the footsteps of her honorable father in the practice of piracy. In fact, I am told that she is a veritable Dragon Lady of Hong Kong. Surely you must have read *Terry and the Pirates** when you were at Smith. I never knew a Smith girl who confined her reading to *Lady Chatterley's Lover.*"

She laughed, but there was a nervous sound to it. "I don't know what you're talking about, Milo."

"Sure you do, honey. You have an organization made up mostly of men who worked for your father. You are using them to steal various historical objects from the mainland and bring them here. It is true that you are either giving these objects into safekeeping for the future or selling them and turning the proceeds over to refugees from the mainland. Since your organization consists of established criminals, I presume you are paying them out of your inheritance. Perhaps it is one way of balancing the books for your father, so that he may rest more comfortably with his ancestors. On the other hand, I'm certain that you have a sincere desire to preserve as much of the culture of the mainland as you can. I admire your purpose, but it is still illegal."

She looked startled. "You mean that ... something like that is common gossip in Hong Kong?"

---

* The Dragon Lady was a notable character in the *Terry and the Pirates* comic strip (1934–1973), based on a twentieth-century pirate named Lai Choi San. The character was a young Chinese woman who led an evil band of pirates, but she became a heroic figure during World War II. She was the source of the term "Dragon Lady," meaning an assertive, powerful woman, usually Asian.

"I don't think so," I said. "I have no connection with common gossip in Hong Kong. I do have access to some very uncommon gossip—which is usually correct. And my guess is that the reason you had to stay home tonight, and the reason you got the phone call, is that you expect some wares to come into Hong Kong tonight."

She was silent for a minute. "Milo, I admire you and I like you—perhaps I even love you, so I must trust you. I don't know where you heard this—and it frightens me—but it is true. I—I felt it was one of the best ways I could use my father's money. You won't do anything about it, will you, Milo? It is important to my people."

"Do you mean will I go to the cops? Of course not. But it is part of what I wanted to talk to you about tonight."

"I don't understand."

"You will, honey," I said. "The men in your organization are experienced—in the legal sense of the word—criminals, aren't they?"

"I suppose so. They worked with my father for years. What they did was against the law, but they are all wonderful people. I will do anything to protect them."

"So would I, Mei," I said gently. "Have you heard, possibly through your men, about medical drugs and business machines of all kinds coming from the United States through Hong Kong and to the mainland?"

She frowned. "I have heard something about it, but nothing definite. Why?"

"That is now my job, and I have almost nothing to go on. I want you to have your men find out whatever they can about it, and also to get some information on five men, if that's possible."

"Who?"

"Shan Chin and Ma Chok, both of Hong Kong."

She had found a pad of paper and was writing down the names.

"And three Americans: Larry Blake and Bernie Henderson, who now live here and have businesses, and Manny Keller, who travels back and forth between America and Hong Kong."

"I will try, Milo. Are you in a hurry?"

"Yes and no. I will explain and then we can stop talking business. I am leaving Hong Kong tomorrow morning. But I expect to return in a few days. If you can have some information by the time I get back, I will be grateful."

"I will try," she said.

"One more thing," I told her. "When I do come back, I will probably be using another name. You see, I am also trusting you. I will be John Milo and not Milo March. Since I am known in certain quarters of Hong Kong, I will have to stay away from there. Quite aside from any business we have, I will want to see you whenever I can, but we will have to stay away from places where I may be recognized. And that will include the police."

"That's no problem," she said. "You can always come here. When do you think you'll be back?"

"I don't really know, Mei. Perhaps in a few days, perhaps longer. I'll call you when I get here. Now that's the end of the business talk. Another martini?"

"Please," she said.

We had two more martinis each, and then went into the next room where dinner was served. To my surprise, it was all French cooking and very good. That and the rest of the evening was pleasure and nothing else.

The operator at the hotel awakened me the next morning. I ordered breakfast from room service and also a morning newspaper. I shaved and showered and did most of my packing while waiting. When the waiter arrived, I took the ice from the orange juice and made myself a V.O. on ice. After breakfast I dressed and finished packing. I had a boy come up for my luggage. I stopped at the desk, settled my bill, and paid for the rental car. Then I took a taxi to the airport.

I don't think I was too surprised when the first person I saw there was Inspector Simmons. I checked my luggage and verified my reservation, then walked over to him. "Going somewhere, Inspector?" I asked pleasantly.

"No," he said. "I merely noticed that you had a reservation on the plane this morning. I didn't believe it, so I came out to see for myself."

"I'm surprised at you, Inspector. I never thought of you as a cynical man. Why this sudden interest in my movements?"

"It seemed likely that you were going to start working in Hong Kong, and we have had some experience with your methods. We know that you went to see Po Hing, which would indicate you were looking for information."

"Po Hing is an old friend of mine and the visit was purely social. Was that your only reason for thinking that I was going to work on a case here?"

"Well," he said stiffly, "your company did go to considerable bother to make certain you took their telephone call, and you did ask me some questions about goods that might be coming through here on their way to the mainland."

I sighed heavily. "Your two points are quite correct, Inspector, but I should like to point out that my company has very little business in Hong Kong. And if there is a case involving goods which come through this port, there are two other things that should be equally obvious to you. If there are any such goods, they must have been stolen in the United States and also insured there, so the case originates there. Obviously it also must be investigated there. Even if the goods are being sent through here, anyone handling this end must be fairly unimportant in the operation. You heard the terms I made with my company. Would it seem logical that they would spend that sort of money to have me chase after errand boys?"

"No, Mr. March," he said glumly, "but my one experience with you indicates that logic cannot be applied to you. I came out to make certain that your reservation was not a trick."

"It's always nice to be seen off on a trip, Inspector. You just stand by and wave to me as we take off. It's been nice seeing you again, old boy."

"I trust it will be the last time, Mr. March. It is not personal, you understand. I find you a rather nice chap, when you're not working. But if we find you working here, I fear that we shall look upon it rather severely."

FOUR

We came down at International Airport in Los Angeles. I checked through customs and then went over to another building and booked myself, as John Milo, on the first flight to San Francisco. When I arrived there, I took a taxi to a little hotel called the Bay Palace. It was not far from the Chinese section. It wasn't quite as fancy as the name implied, but it was still a good hotel. I registered as John Milo.

I was carrying quite a bit of money by this time, some of it in traveler's checks. I went to one of the large banks in the center of the city and cashed these. I used part of the money to open a checking account in the bank and kept the rest of it on me in large bills. Then I went to a public phone booth and put in a call to a bar in Hollywood.

"Is Big Joe Larson there?" I asked when the phone was answered.

"Just a minute."

Big Joe was an old friend of mine. He was in his middle sixties and had been in and around the rackets from Chicago to Los Angeles. He was more or less retired, but he still knew everybody and always knew what was going on.

"Hello," he said a minute later.

"Joe," I said, "don't say my name there or even give a hint of what I'm going to tell you. This is Milo March."

"How are you, cousin?" he said.

"All right, I guess. I'm in San Francisco, staying at the Bay Palace Hotel under the name of John Milo. Got that?"

"Yeah."

"Are you busy?"

"Busy looking for a buck. That's all. The horses shot me in the ass, so I haven't been to the track. What's up?"

"There's an outfit in Los Angeles called the Five Brothers Drug Company. See if you can find out anything about them. In the meantime I'm sending you five bills by Western Union. Take a plane up here and register at the Bay Palace. Call me as soon as you get here—John Milo."

"Got you, cousin."

I hung up and went to look in the phone book. I found the Herman Po Restaurant and took a taxi to it. There were only a few people present. I picked a booth away from the other customers. When the waiter came, I ordered a pot of tea and some little pastries that are filled with meat and seafood.

"Is Herman Po here?" I asked in Cantonese when the waiter brought my food. He looked at the dishes he had just put down. "Is there something wrong?" he asked in the same language.

"No," I said. "I bear a message from a relative of Herman Po's."

"I will see if he is here," he said. He vanished through the door that led to the kitchen.

A few minutes later another man entered through the same door. He was short and plump and looked a little like Po Hing.

"I am Herman Po," he said as he came up to my booth.

"My name is Milo March," I answered. I took the small wooden ball from my pocket and held it out. "I just came from Hong Kong. Po Hing asked me to show this to you."

He took the ball and stared at it, rolling it around with his fingers. "You know Po Hing well?"

"I first met him a number of years ago when we had several visits. This time I saw him three times within the past two days. We have talked much together."

"The waiter," he said, "told me that you speak our language. Do you also read it?"

"Yes."

"Then you know the meaning of the character on this ball?"

"Yes. It is 'Brotherhood.' "

He handed the ball back and sat down across from me. Almost immediately a waiter appeared with another pot of tea and a cup. Another waiter was behind him with a big square bottle and two glasses. He placed them on the table and both waiters left.

"You will join me in a drink?" Herman Po asked.

"I will be honored."

He filled the two glasses and pushed one toward me. "I am the one who is honored," he said, switching to Chinese, "that you are a guest in my humble house." It sounded better in Chinese than it would have in English. Then he laughed and spoke English. "That would really knock Po Hing out if he heard me say it. He never cared much for the old ways. In the meantime, to your good health."

I took a mouthful of whiskey and let it roll around in my mouth before swallowing it. "Lor Mai Tsao," I said.

"You know it," he answered. He seemed pleased by that fact.

"Yes. I've had it many times, but only in Hong Kong."

"It is a good whiskey." He put his glass down and looked at me. "You know, Po Hing does not hand out those wooden balls lightly. Have you ever seen one before?"

"No, but still I did not take the gift lightly. I know that Po Hing does not do things that have no meaning."

He nodded. "How is Hing?"

"Fine. He still seems to be doing well and enjoying himself—except that he misses San Francisco."

"He would. What did Hing tell you about me?"

"That you are his cousin; that you run a fine restaurant; that I would like you—and that you had connections. He did not specify what sort of connections, and I did not ask."

"What kind of connections do you need, Mr. March?"

"I'm not completely certain," I said honestly. "I have a job to do. The job is completely legal, but in order to do it I may have to bend a few laws. The job is partly here and partly in Hong Kong. I believe that the job involves some men who are very big in this country and who also have a brotherhood of sorts. Some of them know me, at least by name. They will not take kindly to the work I am doing. In order to have even a chance of success, it seems obvious to me that I must become another person. I also have to establish certain contacts, but I have other sources for that. Po Hing is a very smart man. I believe that he guessed some of my needs, although we never discussed them, and that is why he suggested I see you."

"What are those needs, Mr. March?"

"In addition to what I need to establish here, I believe that I will be going back to Hong Kong within a few days." I took out the John Milo passport and placed it in front of him. "I already have this as a beginning."

He opened the passport and looked at it. "Hing got this for you?"

"Let us just say that I got it in Hong Kong. The rest is unimportant."

"It is beautiful work," he said, handing it back to me. "What exactly do you want, Mr. March?"

"A complete identity for John Milo. A Social Security card, a couple of credit cards—which I will not use—and a driver's license, from California or any other state, something that will show an address, perhaps here in San Francisco, which will hold up under any casual questioning, perhaps a traffic ticket which has not been paid. Anything that will help to make John Milo a real person—not necessarily completely legitimate, but not too obviously anything else. I would also like a duplicate of this, but in the name of John Milo." I took out my gun permit for the state of California and showed it to him.

He looked it over carefully. "In other words, Mr. March, you want a complete identity established?"

"Yes."

"Would you want the same gun serial number on the permit?"

"No. I would want this one on it." I passed him a slip of paper on which I had written the number of a .38 I owned. It was a legal gun, but it was not registered anywhere.

"Is that all?"

"One more thing. Once these things are delivered, I would like to give you a package to keep for me, with the understanding that you will hand it over only to me or someone who brings you the wooden ball I have. It will contain only those things which constitute my actual identity or possessions which are legally mine."

"It would take about forty-eight hours to obtain all the things you wish."

"That is all right."

"You are probably aware that it will also be expensive?"

"Yes."

"Two thousand dollars," he said. "One-half now, the other on delivery."

"Agreed."

"I will need to keep this permit and will also need your driver's license."

I took out the license and gave it to him. There were ten $100 bills folded beneath it when I gave it to him.

"Very well," he said. "Return in forty-eight hours." He stood up and left the table.

I finished my little cakes and tea, paid the bill, and left.

I stopped off at a nearby bank and opened a small checking account in the name of John Milo. I gave the hotel as my address. I bought some traveler's checks, also in the name of John Milo. Then I went back to the hotel. I had a little talk with the clerk and arranged to have my room put on a monthly basis. I paid him for two months in advance—with a John Milo check. I bought a newspaper and arranged for a bottle of V.O. and some ice to be sent up to my room.

Upstairs, I took off my coat, tie, and shoes, and waited. A waiter soon arrived with the bottle and the ice. I paid him and sent him on his way. I made a drink, then sat down, and wrote two checks on my new Milo March account. Even I was getting confused. One was for two months' rent on my office in New York, the other for two months' rent on my apartment in the same city. I used hotel envelopes, but carefully inked out the name of the hotel. I addressed and sealed these. Then I sat down to enjoy my drink.

I had a second drink while I read the newspaper. After that I went to sleep. I was still tired, and the difference in time hadn't helped much.

I was awakened by the telephone. I glanced at my watch as I reached for the phone. It was almost five o'clock. I picked up the receiver and said hello.

"How are you, cousin?" he said. It was Big Joe.

"All right, I think," I said. "Where are you?"

"In the hotel. Room Four-Ten."

"I'll meet you in the bar in ten minutes," I said.

I hung up and checked the situation. I needed a shave, so I stripped and went into the bathroom. I shaved and showered in less than ten minutes. Then I got dressed. I considered taking a gun with me, but decided I wouldn't need it—unless someone tried to heist me. Only a small amount of my money was in the two bank accounts, so I had around thirty thousand dollars in cash and traveler's checks. I decided it would be safer in my pockets than in the room, so I went down to the bar as I was.

Big Joe was already there with a drink in front of him. He

was enjoying himself. He liked being busy. I loved the big fellow, and I was glad to see him.

"It's good to see you, cousin," I said as I slipped onto the stool next to him.

He looked at me. "You want to talk here?"

"No," I said. There were only a couple of people in the bar, but I still didn't want to talk in public. "We'll go to a restaurant soon and then we can talk."

He had already motioned to the bartender. "Give my father a drink," he said. He already had money on the bar.

"Martini," I said.

We waited until the martini was brought and change made.

"Joe," I said, "I still have more work for you to do, so take it easy on the juice."

"Anything you say, partner," he said.

We each had another drink, then took a taxi to Henry's Fashion. It was a restaurant that served about the best Italian food you could find this side of Rome. We got a table in the corner, and since it was still early there weren't many customers in the place. We ordered drinks.

"Well," I said, after the waiter had brought the drinks and left, "what about the Five Brothers?"

"It's a drug house, all right—medical drugs. It's in downtown L.A. It doesn't seem to do very much business, but it keeps on going. There ain't no five brothers. It's owned by one guy. His name is Eddie Pacelli. He's a front man for the Syndicate, although I don't think it could be proved."

"Is he big enough to do business on an international scale?"

"Hell, no."

"I forgot to ask you this on the phone, but did you ever hear of a private airline called Naples Air Express? Air freight."

He shook his head. "Could maybe ask around."

"I want you to. And I want you to do a few other things."

"Anything, cousin. What's this John Milo thing?"

"It's part of it. I'm working on a case which I think is Syndicate all the way." I knew that even though he was friendly with some of the members, he still hated the Syndicate.

"Those greaseballs are in everything," he said grimly.

"There are a few of them who know me by sight," I said, "but a lot of them know my name. That's the reason for John Milo. I'm going to try to do a little boring from within."

"You can get hurt that way."

"I know. I read it in *True Detective* magazines."

"I didn't bring a piece with me," he said.

"It's all right, Joe. I'll have a piece of my own, but I don't think it'll be needed until much later."

"What do you want me to do?"

I glanced at my watch. "Wait until I make a phone call." I got up and went to a public booth near the rear of the restaurant. I put in a call to Martin Raymond at his home. I got him right away.

"Martin, old boy," I said, "I hope I didn't interrupt your evening martini."

"Not at all," he said. He tried to sound jovial, but it didn't come off too well. "Where are you, Milo?"

"San Francisco at the moment, but I don't expect to be here very long. That's why I'm calling you."

"You've uncovered something?"

"Are you kidding? You hand me nothing and expect all the answers by return mail. No, Martin. I called you for some more expense money."

"What?" he said. He sounded like a boy whose voice is just beginning to change. "I just sent you five thousand dollars plus the agreement about the bonus."

"Martin," I said gently, "I've already spent well over three thousand dollars of your expense money and I haven't even started. In addition, I expect to spend the next several days where you can't get in touch with me and I can't get in touch with you. So send me five thousand dollars tomorrow. Make it payable to my account at the Alexander Bank in San Francisco. You'd better send it by Western Union."

"The Board of Directors will never agree to it." His voice was getting fainter by the minute.

"Martin, have I ever failed to solve a case for you?"

"No, but ..."

"How much insurance is already involved?"

"Well ..."

"They'll agree to it," I said. "Just tell them that if the money doesn't arrive at my bank tomorrow, I quit. Is that clear?"

"Yes, yes, but ..."

I hung up and went back to the table. Joe had already ordered two more drinks.

"First," I told him, "I want you to go to Las Vegas tomorrow. I don't care where you stay, but let me know. Send a telegram to the hotel. You still have friends there?"

"Sure I do."

"Part of your job is to start building up a guy named John

Milo. He's a loner, but he's successful and he's tough. You might even hint that Milo's going to Hong Kong on some sort of scam, but you don't know what it is. I'll show up in a day or two and register at the Desert Flower. I'll run into you accidentally in the game rooms at your hotel—only stay away from the crap table. I'll give you some more money, but it's not for the long shots. I can run out of money."

"Don't worry, cousin. I'll play it cool."

"You'd better," I told him with a grin. "Play the slot machines—the dime ones. Spend the money on buying drinks for the right people."

"Okay."

"Now, if you can, without tipping your hand, see if you can find out anything about Naples Air Express."

He nodded.

"Now something else," I said. "Have you heard anything about hot business machines and drugs going through Los Angeles?"

He was quiet for a minute. "I heard something about the business machines," he said finally, "but I didn't pay much attention. I could probably check up on it by making a couple of phone calls to Hollywood."

"Okay. But make them from a public phone booth here before you go to Vegas. It'll be a big help if you can dig up anything on it. But don't ask your friends in Vegas. I have an idea that they may be part of it."

"All right."

"One final thing. Did you ever hear of Larry Blake, Bernie Henderson, or Manny Keller?"

He thought for a minute, scratching his head. "That Manny Keller, I think he used to be a bagman out of Chicago about ten years ago. He was up on a couple of murder raps, but beat them. I don't remember the other names."

"Check Keller when you get back to L.A. He's now a drug salesman for Five Brothers. Can you get me a sheet if anyone wants to check with the L.A. cops?"

"I think so. I'll have to check."

"Wait until you get back to L.A. Now let's have some dinner."

We had a wonderful Italian dinner with red wine. It was the way Joe liked to live, so he enjoyed it even more than I did—which was saying a lot.

Later we stopped in at a club for a while. By the time we left the club, Joe was gassed. I steered him back to the hotel, led him to his room, and went back down to the bar. I nursed a couple of drinks and brooded. There was a girl at the bar who was in a friendly mood, but I wasn't. I finished my second drink and went to bed.

Joe wasn't feeling too well the next morning. I got him a Bloody Mary and then fed him some breakfast. By then he was in good enough condition to call Vegas and make a reservation and also to call Los Angeles. He was told that a check would be made on the business machines and was told to call back. I impressed on him that he was to make the call from a public phone in Vegas. Then I gave him some money and put him on a plane.

From then on I was just marking time. I had a few drinks, went for a good lunch at a restaurant on the waterfront, then I checked with my bank. Good old Martin had sent through the five thousand dollars. I drew most of it out and then went to another bank and converted it into traveler's checks. I spent most of the afternoon in a bar. That night I had another good dinner and went to the hungry i. I got back to the hotel fairly early, watched television, and worked on the V.O.

The first half of the next day was pretty much the same. Finally, when it seemed time, I went back to Herman Po's restaurant. I ordered a few things to nibble on and a pot of tea. Then I asked for Herman Po.

He came to the booth a few minutes later. The pot of tea and the bottle and two glasses followed fast on his heels. We had the ceremonial drink and indulged in small talk. Then he made a gesture with one hand and a waiter appeared. He was carrying a large manila envelope, which he handed to his boss. When the waiter had left, Herman Po handed it to me.

"You will wish to check it," he said.

"I'm sure it is not necessary," I said. I already had one thousand dollars separated from the rest of my money. I passed it over to him. "I will drop the package off to you later this afternoon."

"That is well," he said. "Hing would not approve—but may you go with the gods."

I went back to the hotel and opened the manila envelope. Everything was there and it was all excellent work. I went downstairs to the nearest men's store. I bought a shirt and had them place it in a box. There was a gift shop next to it. I bought some plain wrapping paper, string, and a chunk of sealing wax.

Upstairs I placed all of my Milo March stuff, including my regular gun, in the box and wrapped and tied it. Then I put sealing wax in various spots and pressed the wooden ball against the wax while it was still soft.

I could have gone to Las Vegas that evening, but I decided to give Joe a little more time. I called and made a reservation for the following day. There was a telegram from Joe with the name of his hotel. I went into my hotel bar and had a couple of drinks, then went back to my room.

I knew what I was going to do, but I didn't know how or what it would get me. But unless Joe turned up something startling—and I doubted that he would—I'd have to find some way of working from inside the gang. It wouldn't be very safe, but it was probably the only way I could get the story. The big question was still how did I get in.

I had a small glass of V.O., then went to sleep. When I awakened it was early evening. I shaved and changed shirts. Then I took my package and went back to Herman Po's. It was still too early for the restaurant to be crowded, so I took a booth. I ordered a drink and dinner, and told the waiter to hold the dinner. I also asked to see his boss.

He came out within a few minutes and sat in my booth. "Everything was satisfactory?" he asked.

"Beautiful work," I said. "I've brought the package I would like you to keep for me." I handed it over the table.

"Fine," he said. "I'll put it in my office safe. When you get back to Hong Kong, say hello to Hing for me."

I promised I would, and he left with my package. There, I thought, went Milo March.

I had a fine dinner. When I started to pay the bill, the waiter told me that I had been a guest of the house. I left him a good tip and went out on the town. I did a little pub crawling, but my heart wasn't in it. Finally, I bought a couple of magazines and went back to the hotel. I got undressed, turned on the TV, made myself a drink, and stretched out on the bed. I read parts of the magazines and watched parts of the TV shows. A stagecoach was lumbering down the road in a late movie when I fell asleep.

Hugh Downs and the *Today Show* woke me up. I phoned room service and ordered breakfast and some ice. While I was waiting I took a quick shower, had one drink out of the V.O. bottle, and put it away in the dresser. If I ever got back to this room, it would be there; if not, someone would be lucky. I got dressed and packed, put in a phone call to Las Vegas, and made sure I had a room reservation at the hotel.

Downstairs, I reminded the clerk that I had paid for the room for the next two months and asked him to hold any mail. Then I went out and took a taxi to the airport.

The Desert Flower Hotel was another of those giant show-places in Vegas. Everything was the best, and the prices weren't too bad because they expected you to do your paying at the tables. I unpacked and put my things away in my room. I knew I couldn't get into the gambling rooms wearing a gun, so I put it and the holster in a dresser drawer. It was a good bet that some of the hotel help would spot it and spread the word.

I went downstairs and had a couple of drinks out on the terrace, where I could indulge in some girl watching. Then I wandered inside and played a slot machine a few times.

There wasn't much action in the gambling rooms yet, but I went in and tried the dice. A girl showed up with a drink on the house. I won about two hundred dollars in ten minutes and quit, tossing the girl a ten-dollar chip.

Back at the desk I inquired about renting a car. Not just a car, a Cadillac. The clerk made a phone call, and twenty minutes later the car was outside. I signed for it. I got in and took a ride out into the country—no particular reason, but I wanted to kill some time and I wanted to seem busy.

When I came back I started up the Strip, stopping in at all the big places. I'd go in and give the dice or the wheel a little play, then move on to the next place. Finally I arrived at the hotel where Joe was staying. I stopped to play a slot machine and then took a look inside. Sure enough, there he was at the crap table.

I wandered into the room and stopped at the roulette table. I made a few bets and lost them, then went over and bought some more chips and headed for the crap table. I noticed that Joe had lost the dice. I stopped suddenly, as if I had just seen him.

"Joe," I exclaimed. "Big Joe! What the hell are you doing here?"

He turned to look at me. So did the other players around the table. "John," he said. "I haven't seen you in months. You been away?"

"Not where you think," I said, "but I've been away. On business." We shook hands and pounded each other on the shoulders. "I thought you would be down in L.A. playing the horses."

"I was, but I decided to come up here for a couple of days. I can lose my money faster here and I don't have to walk up and down those stairs. Where you staying?"

"The Desert Flower. And you?"

"Right here. Say, why don't you have dinner here with me tonight and we can cut up some old touches?"

"Okay," I said.

"You going to take some of the action?"

"Might as well," I said.

I'd noticed that the man with the dice seemed to be starting a run of luck. I walked over and put down a hundred-dollar chip on him. He threw a seven and I let it ride. He threw another seven. I left a hundred on him and picked up the rest. He made three more passes and I was on him. I noticed that Joe had finally put a bet down on him, so I skipped the next play. He threw a double six.

"Wouldn't you know it," Joe growled. "I couldn't pick my own father out of a lineup."

Everyone laughed.

"Quitting already?" Joe asked as I started to edge away from the table.

"No, just taking a breather," I said. "I thought I'd have a drink at the bar and rest my feet."

"I'll join you," he said. "I can't lose anything there but the price of a drink."

I cashed in my chips and we went into the bar. There were a couple of women and a man at one end of the room. We sat at the other end. I ordered a martini and he had a bourbon.

"You broke yet?" I asked him.

"No. I had a little streak of luck the first night I was here, but it seems to be gone. In fact, it started going that first night. But I haven't been spending all my time at the table. I've been busy on—"

"Wait until after we have our drinks," I said. "Then we'll take a ride."

"In a taxi? That's worse than talking at a bar."

"I've got a car."

We finished our drinks and went outside. Just as the boy brought my car, another one pulled in and a short, swarthy man got out. He looked me over in a split second, but I knew he hadn't missed anything.

"Hello, Joe," he said. "You ain't leaving us already?"

"Not as long as I got money in my kick," Joe said. "See you later, Angelo."

I had already tipped the boy and was behind the steering wheel. Joe slid in next to me and we drove off.

"That was Angelo Bacci," he said.

"Who's he?"

"One of the dons in the Syndicate. He owns a piece of the joint where I'm staying and a piece of the one you're at. I used to know him back in the good old days in Chicago."

"Important?"

"Yeah. I've talked you up to him some, and you might meet him tonight when we have dinner."

When we reached the city limits, I slowed down but continued straight ahead into the desert.

"Have you learned anything, Joe?"

"Some, but not too much. That air freight company you

mentioned—it's owned by the Syndicate. They've got five planes and a landing field in Arizona. I guess if you insisted on hiring them to freight something for you, they'd do it, but I think nearly all of their work is Syndicate stuff."

"I thought it might be. How'd you find out?"

"Called a guy I know in Arizona. He ran it down as a favor to me."

"What about the business machines, TV sets, and that stuff?"

"That's a little harder," he said. "There's a lot of action in Los Angeles, but I think that's only part of it. I guess that most of the people involved ain't important at all. Not even part of the mob. I don't know them, but I was told there are two men who run the whole operation and that they are hooked into the mob."

"Any idea who they are?"

"Just their names. I never heard of them before, and I don't imagine they're very high in the Syndicate. They probably get orders on every move. I also heard that most of the stuff is going out of the country, but I don't know where."

"What are their names?"

"Julie Gross and Tony Coffer. I don't think they're seen by more than one or two of the other people involved."

"How about the others?"

"I could make some guesses, but that's all they would be. Some of the action seems to center around a couple of bars on Hollywood Boulevard and one that's farther downtown, east of Vermont Street."

"The Hollywood bars are out for me," I said. "Too much

chance of running into someone who knows me. What's the name of the other bar?"

"The Tippler. It's on the boulevard but below Vermont."

"What's it like?"

"Like a million other bars—some neighborhood trade and a lot of heisters and con men and grifters. What are you looking for? To get next to the gang or just spot them?"

"Get next to them. I want some of them—the more important, the better—to know me and to think I'm safe. Also that I'm not hungry, so they won't think they can hand me a two-bit tip."

He was silent for a minute. "That's a tough one. I can see that you're known to some of the men here, and they'll remember you—if they ever hear of you again. But that won't get you in by itself. How badly do you want to get in?"

"Badly."

"Enough to run the risk of some heat?"

"Yes."

"Well, I can offer you a gamble. There are two men, strictly amateurs, who I think are involved in the business machines. They are also trying to peddle something else. I think it's related, but not part of the Syndicate deal. I might be able to put you in with them, and it might lead to something else."

"What are they trying to peddle?"

"Cutty Sark whiskey. They say it's legal, but the price is so low it probably isn't."

"How's that going to lead to anything else?"

"I also called a cop I know in L.A.," Joe said. "I discovered that there's a police informer who hangs around The Tippler trying to pick up anything at all. If you try to sell the booze around there, he's bound to approach you or report you, and it may bring you into it. It might also get you busted."

"Who are the people involved?"

"The two amateurs are George Carlson and Bill Frame. As soon as we get back to L.A. I'll arrange for you to meet them. Then all you have to do is keep showing up at The Tippler and talk too much. Let them come to you. That's the best I can suggest."

"It might be good enough," I said slowly. "What about the informer?"

"A jerk. He's a little off in the head. A stocky guy with a face like a sick bulldog. He was in the Navy in the war and talks about it all the time. I think the only action he ever saw was in the sick bay. His name is Bob Andrews."

"Okay," I said. I braked to a stop and turned around. "We'll go back to L.A. tomorrow or the next day—separately. In the meantime we'll build up what we can here."

"How's your ID?" he asked.

"Good," I said. "It includes everything. A California gun permit, too."

"You got a piece on you now?"

"Not on me. It's in my room."

"Give me the serial number of the gun and I'll have you a Nevada permit by the time we have dinner."

I fished out the permit and handed it to him. He wrote down the number and gave the permit back to me.

"What if I wear it here? They won't let me into the gaming rooms."

"No. But in most places you can check it. You certainly can at my place. So you can strap it on when we meet for dinner. I'll have the permit by then."

"How much?"

"A bill."

"Okay."

I drove straight back to his hotel, stopped in front of the entrance, and waved the boy away. I pulled out my roll of money and peeled off five bills. "Here's another five hundred, Joe. But go easy on the crap table. Don't try to get rich. This roll won't last forever. I'm going back to my hotel and change and I'll see you in about an hour."

"Okay," he said. He got out of the car and I drove off.

I went straight back to the Desert Flower. I turned the car over to the parking boy and went inside, stopped at the desk, and got my key and then went upstairs. I unlocked the door and stepped inside, closing the door behind me. As I reached for the light switch, since the drapes were drawn, there was suddenly something very hard pressing into my back.

"Just freeze, Milo," a voice said. "Don't move a muscle or you may not have a spine."

FIVE

Freeze was the right word. He had called me Milo. I didn't know whether that meant he knew I was Milo March or he was merely using the last name of John Milo. But there weren't any questions about what was poking in my back. I'd had too many guns shoved against me not to know one when I felt it.

"Now," he said, "move your left hand very carefully and turn on the lights. Then put both hands on top of your head."

I did as he told me.

He quickly patted me on both sides. "Careless of you," he said, "not to carry a piece. But that's a nice little gun you had in the drawer. How come a law-abiding citizen is keeping a gun like that?"

"I'm a gun-collector," I said evenly.

He laughed. "Me, too. Only I've got the gun now. Somebody told me you're carrying a lot of green stuff around with you. Where is it?"

"You mean this is a heist?" I asked.

"What did you expect—a dance?"

It was my turn to laugh. "You should have stayed on your job of parking cars. What do you think I am—a walking poverty program?"

"Shut up," he said tightly. He patted my back pockets, then

the side pockets of my pants. He felt something and reached in, but all he got was a small roll of bills. "You've got more than that," he said. "Where is it?"

"I haven't had time to run off any new bills yet," I said.

He started to reach around in front of me, then changed his mind. "All right," he said. "Keep your hands on top of your head and turn around. But don't make any fast moves."

"I'm too old to move fast," I said. I turned very slowly and then, as I faced him, I said, "But you should have made sure that the drapes were completely closed."

That was just enough to throw him off a little. His eyes flickered toward the windows. Keeping my hands clasped together, I brought them down on the top of his head. At the same time I brought my knee up to meet his face. I could feel the bone in his nose give and his breath come out in a wheeze. The gun dropped from his hand. He tried to straighten up, and I hit him as hard as I could. He skidded across the carpet. I reached him before he stopped sliding, yanked him halfway up, and slapped at his pockets. I found my gun and took it back.

I stepped back and picked up his gun. I took the shells out of it and tossed them on the dresser. I used my handkerchief to wipe my prints off his gun and tossed it to him. He was getting to his feet, blood streaming from his nose. He was a dark little guy with a face like a weasel.

"You're ruining the carpet," I said. "Get up and wipe your nose like a big boy."

He struggled to his feet and glared at me. He said an unprintable word under his breath. He rubbed his hand across his face and it came away crimson.

"Pick up your gun and get the hell out of here," I said.

He looked at me with a stupid expression. "What did you say?" he mumbled. He took another swipe at his bloody nose.

"I said get out."

"You're not going to call the cops?" he asked. He sounded amazed.

"I haven't lost any cops," I said. "Pick up your gun and get out before I decide to take you apart. But make it fast—and stick to parking cars."

He stared at me for another minute, then gingerly picked up his gun and dropped it in his pocket. He sidled toward the door and opened it. He was halfway through it when he stopped and thought. It was obviously a difficult process. He gave me a sickly smile, pulled a handkerchief from his pocket, and rubbed the doorknob. Then he used the handkerchief to close the door.

I picked up my money from the floor and made sure that the door was locked.

Then I went into the bathroom, where I shaved and showered. I got dressed, only this time I strapped on the shoulder holster. I made sure the gun was loaded and slipped it into the holster. I put on my coat and went downstairs.

The boy brought my car and I drove over to Joe's hotel. As I had expected, he was at the dice table. But he had a few chips in front of him, so I decided he was playing above his head.

I edged up behind him. "Knock it off the first time you lose," I said. "It'll still be here later."

He nodded without looking around. He made his point twice, then missed the third time, but kept the dice. He rolled again and this time got snake eyes—two little dots. I nudged him again and this time he backed away from the table.

"I was hot," he muttered as he went over to cash in his chips.

"Not the last time, cousin," I said. "Let's have that dinner and maybe you'll be hot again later."

"Yeah," he said. He tucked the money in his pocket and we headed for the dining room. "This is a good time for dinner. We'll have time to finish before the show goes on."

"How'd you make out?" I asked.

I told you I was hot. I won about four hundred dollars."

"But you cooled off, cousin."

He had a reservation, and when we were seated I noticed that we were in an ideal spot for the show when it went on. A waiter appeared and took our orders for drinks. Neither of us said anything until he had brought them and vanished.

"I see you're carrying the piece," he said then.

"Yeah. I hope you got the permit."

"I got it." He dug a piece of paper out of his pocket and handed it to me. I unfolded it and looked it over. It was made out to John Milo and carried the correct serial number.

"Good," I said. "I think I need this as long as I'm in this town."

"Why?"

"Somebody just tried to heist me."

"What?" he exclaimed. He looked startled. "Who?"

"Somebody tried to heist me," I repeated patiently. "When I went back to my hotel room, there was a guy waiting in the room for me. He put a gun in my back, and he had already taken my gun out of the dresser. He said he wanted my money."

"What happened?"

"I gave him a lesson in manners. I think he also got a broken nose—but it won't hurt his looks any."

"Who was he?"

"How the hell do I know? There wasn't any time for introductions. But I think it was a phony."

"What do you mean?"

"The guy was not only surprised when I didn't call the cops, but I think he was disappointed."

"Could be," he said. "I've been giving you a big buildup. Maybe somebody wanted to run a check. We'll see." We had ordered our dinners but told the waiter to hold them, and were on our third drinks when Joe nudged me. "Here comes Angelo," he said.

I looked up and saw the man I'd noticed earlier in front of the hotel. He was coming toward us, pausing to say hello to various people, but his progress was steady. He finally arrived at our table.

"Everything all right, Joe?" he asked.

"Perfect. Angelo, I want you to meet John Milo, a real jam-up guy. John, this is Angelo Bacci, one of the best." I stood up and shook hands with him.

"Have a drink with us, Angelo," Joe said.

"Okay," he said. He sat down.

He had just made it when a waiter was there with three drinks. He must have been waiting patiently about two tables away.

"Put it on my bill," Joe said.

"No chance," Angelo said. "It's on the house." He looked at me. "You new in town?"

"Not completely," I said. "I've been here before, but not in a long time."

"From the East?"

"I've been there."

"Chicago?"

"I've been there, too."

He smiled, but there was no humor in it. "Do you mind if I ask where you've been recently?"

"No. Hong Kong. And I'm going back soon."

"Why Hong Kong?"

"Business. That's the only reason I go anyplace."

"That's why you're here?"

"No. This is a stopover between San Francisco and Los Angeles."

"Why those two?"

"I sometimes live in San Francisco, and I have business in Los Angeles. Mr. Bacci, Joe says you're all right and that's good enough for me. But I'd like to ask you a question."

"Sure," he said, but his face had become a mask.

"Do you know a local boy who's about five feet six, a hundred and fifty pounds, dark face, black hair, with a face like a weasel? He thinks he's tough but he folds easy."

"Why do you ask?"

"He said he was trying to heist me. I don't think so." He stared at me for a minute, then leaned back, and laughed. "Eddie Lamotti," he said. "Poor Eddie. He'll never learn. He's complaining like hell because you broke his nose while he had his gun on you."

"And it wasn't a heist, was it, Mr. Bacci?"

Joe was kicking me under the table, but I didn't pay any attention.

"No," he said. "Joe's been talking about you. I know Joe a long time, and he's a great guy, but sometimes he gets fooled. I wanted to see what you were made of. I sent Eddie to see you."

"He saw me," I said bluntly. "Joe has also told me that you're a great guy, and I don't think that Joe is fooled as often as some people think. I accept his judgment. I like you. But I don't like your Eddie. And I don't like being pushed around. I do all right, and I'm not looking for any favors. A guy wants to be friendly, I'm willing to be friendly. But the next time a guy tries to heist me or pretends to heist me, he may be carried away. I haven't stayed alive by giving charity. I'm sure you haven't either."

For a minute he looked angry, then his face smoothed out. "You're right," he said. "I'll ask one more question and that's all. What do you want from me?"

"Nothing," I said flatly. "I don't even know anything about you, except that Joe says you're all right. I don't want to know anything else. If you want to say hello to me, I'll like it. If you don't want to, I'll like that too. Now, I'll ask you one more question. If you don't want anything from me, will you have a drink with me?"

He hesitated, then laughed again. "That's fair enough. I'll have a drink with you."

I beckoned the waiter and he brought three drinks. I paid for them. The waiter went away.

I lifted my glass. "Tell Eddie I hope his nose doesn't hurt too much, and if he'll send me the bill I'll pay for it."

Bacci downed his drink at one gulp. "I notice that you're dressed tonight," he said.

"Wouldn't you be, under the circumstances?"

"I guess so. But you know you can't carry that into the game rooms. Do you have a license for it?"

"Two of them. And I know I can't carry them into the gambling rooms. But I presume I can check it."

"Sure. With the cashier." He stood up and looked at Joe. "That's quite a boy you have as a friend," he said. He turned his gaze on me. "I like you, John Milo. You got the kind of guts that most of the boys don't have these days. If you ever get tired of being a loner, come and see me. I'll make you rich. In the meantime, except for the tables, your money is no good here or at the Desert Flower. It's on the house."

He was gone before I could answer, threading his way through the tables, saying hello to people as he went, but not stopping for any length of time.

Joe took a deep breath. "You were really pushing there. He's the wrong kind of man to push. You either shoot a man like that or shut up."

"You're wrong, Joe," I said. "That's the way it used to be, but the mob is more respectable now. They don't like killings, unless it's absolutely necessary—so they push. What do you think he was doing when that punk came up and stuck a gun in my back? He was pushing just to see what I'd do. I pushed back and he liked it."

"Maybe you're right," he said. "I think he did like you, and he'll certainly remember you."

"Somebody better," I said.

We had dinner and watched the show. Joe enjoyed it, but I could see he was itching to get back to the dice table. When it was over, he was on his way. I followed, stopping at the cashier to check my gun and buy some chips.

I sat down at the blackjack game and played for a while. I won a few and lost a few and gave up. I went over to the dice table. Joe had the dice and seemed to be doing pretty good, judging by the chips in front of him. I got into the table and bet with him. I won eight bets and decided it was time to change. I lost two bets, then Joe reverted to his true form and I began winning again.

At last he lost the dice and someone else took them. Joe bet with the new man and began to win again. I also did pretty well, but I finally left and went to the roulette table. I had a lucky streak there, too. Finally, I decided I'd had enough. I got up and went to see how Joe was doing. He was still winning. I caught his eye and he reluctantly left the table.

"Joe," I said, "I want you to go to L.A. early tomorrow."

"Yeah, sure."

"In the meantime you're getting a little gassed, and before you know it, you'll lose all your money. Quit while you're ahead and get some sleep. It is important that you get there tomorrow. I'll be there and I want to talk to you."

"All right," he said unhappily. "I'll play two hundred dollars more and then quit. Honest."

"Okay, Joe. I'll talk to you tomorrow morning in Los Angeles."

I went over to cash in my chips and pick up my gun. Angelo Bacci was standing nearby. "I see you had a good night, Milo," he said.

"Pretty good," I said.

"Leaving so early?"

"Yeah. I have to take off for L.A. tomorrow morning. Maybe I'll be up this way when I come back from the East."

"Look me up if you do," he said.

"I'll do that."

I went out and drove off as soon as the Cadillac was delivered to the front door. Back at the Desert Flower, I stopped at the desk and told them I was checking out in the morning. I paid my bill, including the car rental, and left the car keys with the clerk. I went up to my room. This time I was a little more careful when I opened the door and went in, but there was nobody waiting for me.

I called room service and asked them to send up a bottle of V.O. and some ice.

Then I called the airlines and made a reservation for the next morning. I sat down and checked my winnings for the day. I had placed that money in a separate pocket after deducting what I had started to play with. I had won almost sixteen hundred dollars.

I took off my coat and hung it in the closet. I tossed my tie on the dresser and kicked my shoes off. I turned on the TV, and then the knock came on the door. I went over and let the waiter in. I paid the check and poured a drink as soon as he'd left. I made sure the door was securely locked and that the windows were also, then stretched out on the bed and watched TV.

An hour later I picked up the phone and called Joe's hotel. I asked for him. The operator reported that he didn't answer the phone. I told her to page him in the gambling rooms. In a few minutes he answered. I could tell by his voice he'd been drinking more.

"Joe," I said, "I thought you were going to play two hundred dollars more and then go to bed."

"Hello, cousin," he said. "I was going to go up, but I lost the two hundred. I'll call it quits as soon as I win it back. I feel I've got a hot streak coming up."

"Joe," I said patiently, "the only place you're getting hot is around the collar. How much have you lost?"

"I don't know exactly. But I'm still winning some."

"Okay, quit while you're ahead. I'm sorry, Joe, but this is not a vacation. I gave you money to work for me and you have, but you're not finished yet. I want you in Los Angeles early tomorrow to do some more work. And I want you to have a clear head. This is important to me, Joe, and I'm depending on you."

There was a moment of silence. "You're right, cousin," he said finally. "All my brains turn to oatmeal when I put my belly up against a crap table. All right. I'll cash in my chips and go right up."

"Thanks, Joe."

I hung up and went back to my drink. I waited twenty minutes, then called him again. This time he answered his room phone.

"Good boy, Joe," I said.

"I'm already in bed," he said.

"Did you make a reservation yet?"

"No. I'll make it in the morning."

"I'm on a ten o'clock flight. I don't think we should go on the same plane. Why don't you take an earlier one?"

"All right, cousin."

"And leave a wake-up call."

"Already did," he said. He sounded like he was falling asleep. "Good night, cousin."

I hung up and poured another drink. I picked up the phone and left a call for myself. Then I finished the drink and went to sleep.

The phone woke me up. I thanked the operator, then called room service and ordered breakfast. I shaved and showered while waiting. The waiter wheeled in the table a few minutes later. I paid the bill and he left. I took an ice cube out of the orange juice and had a drink before I tackled the scrambled eggs and bacon. I got dressed and packed. This time I included the bottle of V.O.

I phoned the desk and asked them to call a taxi for me. Then I put in a call to Joe's hotel. I was told he had already checked out. I had a bellhop come up for my luggage. I stopped at the desk long enough to pay for the extra phone calls, then went out to the waiting taxi.

When we came down at International Airport, I grabbed a porter and had him take my luggage out to a taxi. I told the driver to take me to Hollywood, then go down Hollywood Boulevard past Vermont and I'd tell him where to stop. He nodded and we took off.

As soon as we'd passed Vermont, I kept a sharp watch

on the street. Finally I spotted The Tippler bar. Two blocks beyond it there was one of those supermotels that you find in California. I told the driver to stop there. I had him wait until I was sure I could get what I wanted. I could. It was a large ground-floor room with a kitchen. There wasn't a back door, but there was a large window in the kitchen which opened out at the rear of the motel—in the event I had to make a quick escape sometime. I took it. The owners agreed to move in a color TV set for an extra five dollars a week. I signed the register and paid a week in advance. Then I paid off the cab driver and carried my luggage inside. I unpacked and went out on the street. I found a public phone booth not far away. I phoned a bar up near Western Avenue and asked for Joe Larson.

He came on the phone at once. He didn't sound too good, but at least he was there.

"How do you feel?" I asked.

"I'm a sick mother," he said. "How are you, cousin?"

"All right, I guess. How did you end up financially?"

"A little ahead," he said, lowering his voice. I knew that was so no one in the bar would hear him. "Where are you?"

"I'm registered in the Native Son Motel on the Boulevard. About two blocks from the bar you told me about. I'm calling from a public phone, but you can reach me at the motel—John Milo. Now I'm going to check in at The Tippler. Set up the meeting with the two guys whenever you can, but be careful where. The sooner the better, but you'd better give me a day or two to get established. Keep in touch."

"Okay."

I hung up and walked to The Tippler. It was a large room with a long bar. Against one wall there was a piano bar. There was a television set in the wall up near the ceiling and, of course, the usual jukebox. Five customers were in the place. Four of them were sitting near each other in the middle of the bar. They looked like workers. The fifth guy sat at the end of the bar, nursing a beer. The minute I saw him, I was reminded of Joe's description of the police informer. He was a husky guy, maybe in his early forties, with arms that were just a little bit too short. And his face did look like a sick bulldog's.

The bartender came over when I sat down about three stools from the sick bulldog. I ordered a V.O. with water backed, unbuttoned my jacket, and lit a cigarette. I knew that the bartender would spot the strap of my shoulder holster. He brought the drink, took my money, and brought back the change. He looked at me without any expression.

"You a cop?" he asked.

"Do I look like a cop?" I countered.

He shrugged. "Some cops look like cops and some look like ballet dancers."

"Which do I look like?" I asked.

"Look, Mac, I didn't say you looked like anything. I asked you a simple question. Are you a cop?"

I reached into my pocket and pulled out the California gun permit. I threw it on the bar. "I'm not a cop and I'm not pulling a heist. Take a look for yourself and write it down. And I came in for a drink—not conversation."

He picked up the permit and looked at it. Then he handed it back to me. "I just asked," he said, "that's all."

"So you asked. I answered. Okay?"

"Okay," he said, and retreated.

Nobody had paid any attention to the exchange except the sick bulldog. But he didn't say anything and I didn't look at him. I sipped my drink until it was finished. I motioned to the bartender. He came down. "Give the bar a drink," I said. "Count yourself in."

He made the drinks without comment. The five customers raised their drinks in a silent toast and I responded in kind. The bartender gave himself a bottle of beer and morosely attacked it.

Another customer came in. He was a young fellow wearing a loud sports jacket. He ordered a glass of beer and started sipping it. I made myself a bet that he was a cop. I doubled the bet when the bartender started talking to him, and I saw him shoot one glance in my direction. I concentrated on my drink.

The bartender retreated to the vicinity of the cash register. The young man took another sip of his drink and stood up. His beer and his change were on the bar, so he was obviously going to the men's room. I didn't even look around. I took out a cigarette and lit it as he started walking toward the back of the bar.

I heard his footsteps stop behind me and I was aware that everybody in the bar, including the bartender, was watching while pretending they weren't. I took another swallow of my drink, puffed on my cigarette, and stared at the ceiling. An arm came around my right shoulder and there was an open wallet in the hand. There was a badge in the wallet and a card with a photograph of the nice young man.

"Police," the voice said. "Just sit still."

"What else?" I asked without looking around. "I very seldom dance by myself. Besides, there's no music. But you're wasting your time. I never buy tickets to the policemen's ball. It's against my religion."

The wallet disappeared and something hard was pressed against my back. It was a familiar feeling.

"Put your hands on top of your head," he said.

SIX

There was definitely something familiar about it. I smiled as I put my hands on my head. He reached around and took the gun from my shoulder holster.

"It's difficult," I said, "to drink in this position, and that's what I came in for. Be careful with the gun. It's loaded, and I wouldn't want you to hurt yourself."

"How come you're carrying a gun?"

"Because I have a permit. Want to see it?"

"All right," he said uncertainly. "But don't make any fast moves."

"Don't worry. I'm too old for fast moves." I reached in my pocket and got out my ID folder. I opened it to the California license and passed it back to him.

"A license for the whole state," he said. He sounded unhappy.

"When did you graduate from the academy, officer?" I asked.

"Last—" he started, then broke off. "Why do you have a license to carry a gun?"

"I'm the last of the big spenders," I said.

"What does that mean?"

"May I reach into my pocket?"

"Okay, but move slowly," he said.

I reached into my pocket and brought out my roll. "This is what it means. It's called money."

"Where'd you get it?"

"I inherited it from an uncle who was a dirty old man. He'd always wanted to have a nephew who was a dirty young man."

"I could take you in," he said. He sounded frustrated.

"On what charge?" I asked gently.

"Well … disturbing the peace."

"With six witnesses? Okay. You got a dime, officer?"

"Why?"

"So I can call my lawyer without waking the bartender up to make change."

"You live in San Francisco?" he asked, changing the subject.

"Yes."

"What are you doing in Los Angeles?"

"Trying to have a quiet drink. I never knew it was so difficult."

"All right," he said angrily. He put the gun on the bar next to my hand. "Just don't go waving it around."

"I wasn't," I said mildly. "You were waving it around." He marched back to the end of the bar, grabbed up his change, and left without finishing his beer. When he was gone, everybody laughed except the bartender.

I finished my drink and ordered another. The bartender brought it and took my money without saying anything.

"That was pretty smart," a voice said. I realized it was the sick bulldog. "You a Navy man?"

"I can't stand water," I said.

"Air Force?"

"I don't care much for air either. You see one cloud, you've seen them all."

"Army?"

"I hate walking."

"Weren't you in the War?" His voice put the capital in the word.

"Sure. I was in the K-9 regiment. I barked."

He laughed because he didn't know what else to do. "I'm Bob Andrews," he said. That was the name Joe had given me.

"That's nice," I said.

"What's your name?" he asked. He was persistent.

"John Milo."

"What's your racket?" he asked.

"Minding my own business. What's yours?"

"I was in the Navy for fifteen years," he said, making it sound as if he'd been an admiral. "Since then I've been staying around here, making a buck here and there."

"What's your rate?"

"I don't know what you mean."

"How much do you make an hour?"

He gave me a wise-guy smile. "It depends on what kind of score it is."

"Would you work for five dollars an hour?"

"I might if it was easy work."

I pulled out my money and found a five-dollar bill. I tossed it over to him. "All right. You're hired. Keep quiet for an hour."

He didn't like it, but he took the five dollars. I ordered

another drink for myself. When the bartender brought it, I put five dollars and sixty-five cents on the bar. "The five dollars is for you and your partner," I said.

He was surprised. "My partner?"

"The cop. You'd make a great team if vaudeville weren't dead."

I finished my drink in one gulp and walked out. I figured I'd made enough of a hit for one day.

I went back to the motel. I looked through the Yellow Pages—my fingers didn't want to run through them—and called a car rental place. I told them I wanted a new Cadillac. I gave them my name and where I was staying. They wanted to know about credit cards. I told them that I had credit cards, and named them, but said that I preferred to make a cash deposit. They said it would be rather high, and named a figure. I said fine and would they deliver it immediately.

They did—although they obviously took a dim view of anyone who didn't want to use his credit cards. But they took the money and gave me a receipt and took off.

I got in the car and drove downtown. I parked in a lot on Main Street and went into a restaurant right next to it. I was right about one thing. Joe was there. The place was full of cops, and he was buying drinks for all of them. I said hello to the owner when Joe introduced me, and retreated to a booth. I ordered a martini and some lunch.

Joe came over and I told him what had happened at The Tippler. He was amused, as I knew he would be. He wanted to introduce me to various people, but I decided it was better if he didn't. He said he'd fix it up for me to meet Frame and

Carlson in two days. I said that would be fine. I had a good lunch and took off, went back to the motel, had a drink out of my bottle, and went to sleep.

That evening I went back to The Tippler. It was a different bartender and different customers—except that the sick bulldog was there. He said hello and I nodded, and that was the end of it. I had a few drinks, talked to the bartender, and finally left. I noticed that the sick bulldog was outside, watching me as I drove away in the Cadillac. I went south and east until I saw a restaurant that looked pretty good, and stopped.

I got a table and ordered a drink. Then I went to the phone booth. I called Herman Po in San Francisco.

"I want to send a message to Po Hing," I said when I got him on the phone, "but I don't want anyone else to understand it if they should happen to see it."

"Do you speak Mandarin?" he asked in that language.

"Yes."

"Then use it. I don't think it is necessary, but the man who fears the tiger does not go into the jungle. I can send such a message if it's not too complicated."

"All I want to say is: Make trouble for the courier, but only enough to make it seem that he might be a bad risk."

"That will be easy."

"I will settle with you when I return."

"Not necessary. I will add a personal message so you can have free ride in the oxcart."

"I'll see you anyway," I said, and hung up.

I ate dinner and then went to a movie. Afterward, I stopped in at The Tippler again. I went home about midnight, worked on the V.O., and watched television. I went to sleep after the late show.*

The next morning I made a cup of instant coffee in the kitchen and had it with a shot of V.O. Then I felt up to facing the daylight—what there was of it filtering through the smog. I had breakfast in a little place not far from the motel, then retired to The Tippler. By the end of the day I was practically a fixture there, which was the way I wanted it.

That evening Joe called me at the motel. "You'll meet the two guys tomorrow," he said, "in Glendale. I'll go out with you. Have you got a car?"

"Yes."

"I'll come down to your motel about twelve o'clock and we'll drive out. All right?"

"Fine," I said.

That night I took a chance and went uptown for dinner. I picked a place on Sunset where I'd never gone before, and I guess it was safe enough. I didn't see anyone I knew. After dinner I went back to The Tippler. Even the regulars were beginning to say hello to me. I closed the place up, then went back to the motel to the V.O. and television. I was beginning to get bored.

I was back at The Tippler the following morning, but I left in time to be at the motel when Joe arrived. We got into the Cadillac and headed for Glendale.

We ended up at a little bar and restaurant. I parked in the rear of it and we went in. There were several men at the bar, but one man was sitting at the end by himself.

---

* In the 1960s there was a syndicated movie show on TV called *The Late Show*. After 11:30 p.m. there was also a *Late, Late Show*.

"There's one of them," Joe said, nudging me.

He looked just like a character on Madison Avenue in New York. We went over to him.

"Hello, Bill," Joe said.

The man looked around and smiled. "Hello, Joe," he said. "George couldn't make it today."

"That's okay," Joe said. "Bill, this is John Milo, the guy I told you about. John, this is Bill Frame."

We shook hands. "Let's move to a table," he said. "We can talk there while we're having lunch."

We moved over to a table in the corner. Joe and I ordered drinks from the one girl who was waiting on tables.

"Like I told you," Joe said after the drinks were delivered, "John is the one guy who can help you move the stuff."

"I hope so," he said.

"Suppose you tell me about it," I suggested.

He took a deep breath. "It's eight hundred cases of Cutty Sark. We want to sell it in one bunch and not split it up."

"Hot?" I asked.

He shook his head. "It's in a bonded warehouse and has all the seals on it. It can be examined in the warehouse and will be delivered from there."

"Then what's the problem?" I asked bluntly.

"One company has the franchise for all Cutty Sark in this area," he said. "This shipment was meant for Arizona and was sent here by mistake, to a friend of mine who operates a restaurant. It's more Cutty Sark than he can use or even store, and he doesn't dare try to sell it openly. In fact, the only person who can probably buy it is someone with three or four restaurants and bars and with storage space. He will not be breaking any law by buying it, but if the franchise holder does find out about it, the man might have trouble getting deliveries of Cutty Sark in the future. That's the problem."

"I see. How much a case?"

"We want thirty-five dollars a case. You can have all over that you can get."

The price was right, but I wondered about the rest of it. "You're sure it can be examined in the warehouse?"

"Positive."

"What happens if I get a buyer?"

"Call me." He handed me a card with his name and phone number on it. "I'll set up the date for the man to see it in the warehouse. We'll deliver wherever he wants it."

"Okay," I said. I didn't care too much about the deal if it would accomplish what I wanted. "How many people are trying to sell it?"

"Just my partner and myself, but we're busy with our own business, and we don't know too many places that can handle as much as eight hundred cases. We won't give it to anyone else unless you can't sell it within the next week or so. It has to be moved fairly quickly or the warehouse charges will send the price up."

"Okay," I said. I put the card away in my pocket. "I'll phone you soon."

We had lunch, and Joe and I left. I dropped him off at Hollywood and Western and went on down to The Tippler. The regular afternoon bartender was on duty. There weren't many customers there, although the sick bulldog was. He was sitting at the end of the bar as usual and said hello. I nodded my head and ordered a drink.

"When does the owner come in?" I asked when the bartender brought me my change.

"I'm the owner," he said. "What do you want?"

"Maybe nothing. Do you mind if I ask you another question?"

"I don't mind if you ask."

"Do you own any other places, or is this the only one?"

"I own three others. You want to buy this one?"

"Not right now. I'd rather sell something."

"What?"

"Eight hundred cases of Cutty Sark."

"That's a lot of booze. Hot?"

"No," I said. "At least, I'm told it isn't. I haven't seen it, but I'm told that it can be examined in a bonded warehouse, and I don't think they take hot goods."

"How much?"

"Forty dollars a case."

I told him the story I'd heard. "It could be, I guess," he said when I'd finished. "I don't know whether I can find storage space for that much or not. I'll have to check around. You're sure I can go to the warehouse to examine it?"

"That's what I'm told. And you can examine as many cases as you want to at random."

"It's a good buy if everything checks out," he said. "I'll think about it. Where can I reach you?"

"I'm in here every day," I said. "My name is John Milo. You can leave word that you want to see me with any of your bartenders."

"Okay," he said. He moved away to serve a new customer. I sipped my drink and waited, and then I got the move I'd expected. The sick bulldog picked up his beer and moved down to the stool next to mine.

"I hope you don't mind," he said.

"What's the difference? It's a free country."

"I'd like to talk to you for a couple of minutes."

"I've noticed you like to talk," I said. "Go ahead. But not about the Navy. I get seasick."

"I couldn't help but hear what you were saying to Phil," he said, "about the Cutty Sark. I might know somebody who'd take all of it right away quick. Interested?"

"It's for sale to anybody who has the cash."

"What would be in it for me?"

I looked at him. "A buck a case—if it's a quick sale."

"It'll be a quick sale." He lit a cigarette and gave me a fast look. "What if I get him to go for forty-three a case? Do I get the three?"

"Sure—if it's quick."

He slid off the stool and went to the other end of the bar where there was a public phone on the wall. The owner-bartender came down and emptied my ashtray.

"Maybe I'm sticking my neck out," he said, "but watch yourself. That guy's trouble."

"I figured, but he keeps talking and I can't make out any way to stop him unless I slug him, and that wouldn't be any good for your paper."

"You can say that again. Thanks." He took a couple of swipes at the bar with a rag. "But if he's part of the deal, I don't want anything to do with it."

"He's not part. He wants to stick his nose into it, but that's all. I don't like his nose."

Phil nodded and left. I watched the guy at the phone. I wondered if he was being a fink or trying to moonlight a little. It was hard to tell about a guy like that.

Finally he left the receiver hanging and came back to me. "Can you be here at twelve tomorrow?"

"I can be here."

He went back to the phone and talked for another minute. Then he hung up and came back to me. "He'll meet us here at twelve tomorrow."

"Who is he?"

"A businessman. Has his own fleet of trucks. Everything. Has his own space at a truck dock down on Alameda."

"That's nice. Does he have a name?"

"Sure. Frank."

"Just Frank. No last name, no parents?"

"Look, you got it all wrong," he said. "He'll buy the stuff if it's legitimate. He'll maybe use two hundred cases for Christmas presents. The rest he'll truck out of this area where he can sell it without any trouble. But maybe the two hundred cases that he uses for presents won't show on his books. So he'd rather not have you or anybody else know that's what he's doing."

"Great," I said. "So he's Frank. You're Bob. And I'm John, or, if he prefers, he can just call me baby. I'll see you at twelve tomorrow. Tell Frank baby that he gets ten minutes and no more." I got up and walked out. I didn't even finish my drink.

I got in the car and drove to Burbank. I cruised around until

I found a place that looked decent, went in, and had a martini and some dinner. Then I sat around and drank most of the evening. I had company. I met two nice guys who also liked to drink. One was named Jack De Monbrun and the other Chuck Bean.* They didn't want to buy anything or sell anything. So we drank and told dirty stories, and about midnight I steered the Cadillac over the pass and back to Hollywood. I made it to the motel and went to bed.

The next day I deliberately stayed away from The Tippler in the morning and got there a few minutes late. Bob Andrews, whom I still thought of as the sick bulldog, was sitting at the bar with another man. He looked to be about forty, a nice-looking guy dressed in casual clothes. Bob saw me and motioned me to join them. I went over.

"John, this is Frank," he said. We shook hands and I ordered a martini. I took the stool next to Frank. He didn't saying until I had my drink.

"Bob says you have eight hundred cases of Cutty Sark," he said.

"I don't have them, but I know about them."

"Forty-three dollars a case?"

"Yes."

"And I can examine them in the warehouse?"

"That's what I'm told."

"Okay. How soon can we go?"

"I'll make a phone call." I went to the phone on the wall and called Bill Frame. I told him that I had somebody who

---

* It is likely that these two names are friends of the author, who enjoyed inserting such private "jokes" in his novels. The tipoff here is the distinctive nature of the names and the characters' irrelevance to the story.

wanted to see the whiskey right away. He said he'd have to call me back. I gave him the number and went over to where they were sitting.

"He's calling me back," I said.

We waited. Bob kept talking to the other guy, bragging about smart deals he had pulled and how great it had been in the Navy. He annoyed me, but I didn't say anything.

The phone on the wall rang. I walked over and answered it. It was Bill Frame.

"We can't make it today. The guy who owns the liquor is busy. See if you can make it tomorrow. About one o'clock will be fine. Let me know where you will be and I'll pick you up then."

"Okay," I said. I went down again to where they were sitting. "The owner can't make it today. But you can see it definitely tomorrow at one o'clock."

"Why can't we see it today?" Bob demanded. "Don't they want to sell it?"

"I would presume," I said, "that the man has other things to do than just sit around all day waiting for us to phone."

"Well, it's a hell of a way to do things. What's the number? I'll call him."

"You're trying to be a big man all of a sudden," I said. "Better wait until you grow some more. That's the way the man says it's to be, so that's the way it's going to be."

"Tomorrow's all right," Frank said. "Look, I don't have to come back here. See if they can deliver it to a trucking dock on Alameda tomorrow. I can examine it there on the truck, and if it's all right you'll get the money and we'll unload it. Murphy's Trucking, Dock Fourteen." I went back to the phone again. Bill Frame said that was all right and the truck would be there at one o'clock, and then I could come back with the money.

I told Frank that the truck would be there at one. He nodded. "There's a restaurant near there called the Alameda Gem. I'll meet you there at the parking lot at twelve-thirty. My car's a red Cadillac."

"Mine's a white one," I said.

He shook hands and left. Bob wanted to start talking, but I cut him off. I told him I'd pick him up the next day at noon, and then I left. I drove downtown and had lunch at my favorite spot.

The following day I stopped at The Tippler and picked up Bob Andrews. We drove downtown, then across Alameda until we came to the restaurant. I pulled into the parking lot and parked next to the red Cadillac.

Frank put his head out of the window. "Follow me," he said.

We drove a couple of blocks and then pulled into a large trucking dock. There was a long platform with spaces for about thirty trucks on each side. We parked to one side, out of the path of the trucks, and went up on the platform. Bob Andrews kept walking back and forth, swinging his arms, and talking. Neither of us paid any attention to him.

It was almost one o'clock. "What happens," I asked Frank, "when you've examined the whiskey and find it's all right?"

"I'll call my partner," he said. "He's only a couple of blocks from here and has the money with him. I will tell you where to go to meet him, and he'll give you the money and you'll give him a receipt. While that is taking place, I'll get the truck unloaded and then our truck will come in later to pick it up."

"Why doesn't your partner come here and wait with us?"

He smiled. "He's carrying a lot of money in cash. And I might point out that you're carrying a gun."

"I'm also carrying as much money in cash as your partner is. I'm also carrying a permit for the gun."

"I didn't mean anything by it," he said, "but when there's that much money in a deal, I believe in being careful."

"So do I," I said.

One o'clock came and no truck. One-thirty and still no truck. Finally it was almost two o'clock, and Frank was getting restless.

"What kind of Mickey Mouse deal is this?" he said. "I'm going to call my partner and tell him to take the money back to the bank."

"I'll go call them," I said.

I walked up to the other end of the platform where there was a phone booth and called Bill Frame.

"What's happened?" I asked.

"The truck broke down," he said, "and I didn't know how to get in touch with you. It had to be towed back to the warehouse. I don't think we can get another truck in time for today."

"The customer's a little annoyed, and I don't know if he'll stand still for it or not."

"Tell him we'll deliver it tomorrow, the same time."

"Okay."

I went back to the platform and told Frank. "All right," he said. "We'll give them one more chance. I'll meet you here tomorrow. But this time I want the principals here. It's no good if you have to run and make a phone call every time something goes wrong."

He got in his car and left.

I drove Bob back to The Tippler and told him I'd pick him up the next day. I'd had enough of his talk, so I didn't stop. I went back to the motel and called Bill Frame from there. I told him what had happened and he said he'd be at the dock.

The next day we drove straight to the trucking dock. Frank was already there. We started waiting again. A few minutes later two cars drove in at the same time. Bill Frame was in one of them. The other guy almost looked like his twin. He turned out to be George Carlson. Everybody was introduced and they said the truck was on its way.

Then the sick bulldog turned to Bill Frame and said, "Do you fellows have anything else for sale? Frank here is interested."

Bill Frame said, "Yes."

At that point I went for a walk. This was obviously the contact I needed, but at least then I didn't want to know too much about it. I liked Frank, but something about him made me nervous, and I already knew that Bob Andrews was a police informer. So I went to the other end of the platform, smoked a couple of cigarettes, and watched a truck unload. It was very exciting.

By the time I walked back down to where the rest of them were, we had more company. This time, I thought, we had hit pay dirt. There were two guys who had also arrived in separate cars. One was driving a new Cadillac, the other a new Lincoln Continental. Both of them had the look of successful hoods. They were in serious conversation with Frank and Bob, so again, I stayed away.

The truck still hadn't arrived, but apparently a decision was made. Bill Frame must have made another phone call, because they said there was some delay about the delivery. Frank and Bob were going off with the two men who had just arrived to look at something. Bill Frame, George Carlson, and I were to go to the Alameda Gem and wait for phone calls. Somebody was to call us about the liquor delivery, and Frank or Bob would call us when they were ready to leave Hollywood.

We made a three-car parade down Alameda to the Gem. We went into the small bar and had a couple of slow drinks. Then we moved to a table in the restaurant part, where we had a few more drinks before we ordered lunch. We were just about ready for coffee and dessert when there was a phone call for me.

It was Bob Andrews. "Everything is fine here," he said. "Did you hear about the whiskey?"

"No."

"What the hell is wrong with them?" he demanded.

"Maybe he didn't have a dime to make the call," I said.

He didn't have a sense of humor. "We'll see you soon," he said, and hung up.

I went back to the table and reported the conversation. All three of us were getting tired of waiting around. We finished coffee and dessert and ordered more coffee. I had some brandy with mine.

We were on our third cups of coffee when there were some newcomers. Two men came in the front way, and I was aware that a man had come up behind me. One of the men put his open wallet in front of us. There was a badge in it.

"Police," he said. At the same time he produced a gun. "Stand up and raise your hands."

SEVEN

My first thought was of the sick bulldog. I stood up and raised my hands. The man behind me quickly found my gun and took it. The other detectives patted the two men with me, but didn't find anything.

"What is this?" I asked. "Are you charging us with something?"

"Yeah," said the man behind me, "with keeping bad company. Put your hands behind your back."

I did as he told me and he snapped handcuffs on my wrists. They hurt as they bit into the flesh.

"Why the hell do you have to have such big wrists?" he asked.

"Sorry," I said. "If I'd known you were coming, I'd have reduced."

"Don't be smart," he said. "Let's go."

The others were also handcuffed. We marched out of the restaurant escorted by the three detectives. We had already paid the check, so no one did anything but stare at us, as if they thought the L.A. police had just rounded up the entire Mafia.

We were put in the rear seat of a police car and then we took off. It's a little painful to sit in a car with your hands cuffed behind you.

We finally arrived at a police station and were escorted inside. I was led—or pushed—to a large table. The handcuffs were removed and I was told to sit down. Then one wrist was cuffed to the chair. I was left there.

After a minute I looked around. I saw Bob Andrews, George Carlson, Bill Frame, one of the two men who had shown up at the trucking dock, and several other people. But I was the only one still handcuffed. Maybe it was supposed to be an honor.

Finally two detectives came over to me. "What's your name?" one of them asked.

"John Milo."

"Empty out your pockets."

Using one hand, I did as he told me. The two of them looked at the roll of money and the traveler's checks. One of them whistled. "You can put the money back in your pocket," he said.

They started going through everything else I had had in my pockets. "What do you know," one of them said, "he's even got a permit for that gun we found on him."

"How come you got a gun permit?" the other one asked me.

"The money," I said. "I don't like being robbed."

"How come you carry so much money?"

"I don't trust banks. They get robbed, too."

"All right. What were you doing at that restaurant?"

"I thought it was obvious. I was having lunch. By the way, what am I charged with?"

"I didn't hear anyone say you were charged with anything."

"You mean it's just a social visit? In that case I'll leave, if you don't mind. I'm particular about who I associate with."

"A wise guy," he said. "All right, put the stuff back in your pockets. Somebody will talk to you soon." He got up and left.

I stayed where I was. The handcuffs made it necessary. An office door opened and Frank came out with two detectives. He was angrily demanding to be allowed to call his attorney. The cops finally cuffed him and then took him out. The whole scene was overacted for my benefit, I thought, and I knew why I had felt nervous about him.

Others kept going into the office and coming out. As soon as they came out, they departed. The only one I didn't see go in there was Bob Andrews. But he kept going in and out of another office.

Finally, everyone except me had been called in. I had been there about four hours.

A detective came over and took the cuffs off. "Go in there," he said, pointing to the busiest office. I walked over and went in. There were two detectives there, one sitting behind a desk.

"Well, John," said the one behind the desk, "I left you until last because I figured you're a smart guy and you'll tell me the truth. Now, what's your story?"

"First," I said, "what am I charged with?"

"Nothing, so far," he said pleasantly. "Tell us the truth and maybe you'll just walk out of here."

"The truth about what? You haven't told me what I'm being questioned about."

"Well, start off by telling us what you were doing down on Alameda."

"I was having lunch with Mr. Frame and Mr. Carlson concerning a business proposition. Although I have met them only recently, I understand they are legitimate businessmen and our talk was about legitimate business." I noticed that there was a large glass window between this office and the one next door and that the sick bulldog was standing at the window showing great interest in what we were saying.

"Then why did you meet them at the trucking dock?" the detective asked.

"I wanted to have lunch with them today. I was told that they use considerable trucking in their regular business and that they had to be there to arrange for some shipment. They suggested that I meet them there and we would then go on to lunch. I did and we did."

The detective had been taking notes. Suddenly he threw the pencil down in pretended anger. "I guess I made a mistake," he said. "I thought you were an honest man. Now I think you're a damned liar."

I smiled. "We haven't really met. Do you have a name and a title?"

"Gilbey. Sergeant Gilbey."

"Well, Sergeant, you certainly have a right to your opinion. But I also have rights. Now, I insist that I be granted those rights. If you're going to book me, do so. I also have the right to get a lawyer. I want to do so."

"What do you want a lawyer for? You know they're all a bunch of crooks."

"Maybe," I said, "but at least he'll be *my* crook. What about my phone call?"

"You can make that downtown. Come on."

The three of us walked out of the office. As soon as we were outside they put handcuffs on me again. Frame and Carlson were also still waiting. They put us all in the back of a car and drove us downtown.

At police headquarters they herded us into one of the elevators and upstairs, where there were more cops. We were lined up at a counter.

One of the detectives slapped a gun on the counter in front of me. "This is his gun," he said to the man behind the counter. "Be sure to respect his rights and include it in the receipt. He has a permit for it."

The other cop looked at me. "Empty out your pockets," he said.

I did as he told me. He looked at the money and whistled. "Pretty rich, ain't you?"

"I inherited it from an uncle who was a cop," I said. "Just be sure that you count it correctly and include it in the receipt."

He went through everything, writing down each item on a printed form. It took him a long time to count the money, and I wasn't sure he could count that high. But he finally finished and looked at me. "I make it thirty-one thousand, two hundred and seventy-two dollars and sixty-five cents. Is that right?"

"It's close enough," I said. "Anything that spills over from that is yours."

"Step in here," one of the other cops said to me. I was led into the next room where they took some pictures of me—one full face and one in profile. Boy, I thought, was everybody going to be surprised when they ran the picture and my prints through the FBI. I went back to the counter.

"Take off your clothes," the detective said, "and hand them to me one piece at a time."

I did as I was told. He felt each piece of clothing and then tossed it on the counter. Finally I was standing there stark naked.

"Face me," he said.

I did.

"Open your mouth."

I opened my mouth and he peered inside.

"Raise your arms."

I did.

"Lift up your scrotum."

I obeyed. "I didn't know you cared," I said.

He ignored me. "Turn around and bend over, spreading your cheeks."

I did as he told me and then he said, "All right. You can put on your shorts. Sign the receipt for your things." I put on my shorts and faced the detective on the other side of the counter. He shoved the form and a pen in front of me. I noticed that he had already signed it. I read it over carefully. "It says thirty-one thousand, two hundred and seventy dollars."

"I'm giving you two dollars and sixty-five cents, your package of cigarettes, and a pack of matches," he said.

"Gee, that's great," I said. I signed, then scooped up the money and the cigarettes.

"Pick up your clothes and go through that door," the detective said. He was pointing to a barred door.

"When do I get to make my phone call?" I asked.

"After you're booked. Go on."

I picked up my clothes and went to the barred door. A guard inside opened it.

"Go in there," he said, pointing to a glass-walled room, "and take a shower."

I went inside. There were two bare rooms. The first one had a bench. I put my clothes on it. The other room had two shower nozzles. They were already spurting water. I took off my shorts and went under the shower. When I came out there was an old beat-up towel on the bench. I rubbed myself dry and put on my clothes. Then I stepped outside.

"Sit there," a guard said. He pointed to a chair and a table. I sat down. He brought me paper and a pen. I had to write my name, age, address, and also mark which letter followed which one in the alphabet. I guess it was an IQ test.

After that I was taken over to a counter and fingerprinted.

"Now can I make my phone call?" I asked.

"Sure. If you got a dime. The phone's right there."

"Where am I?" I asked.

"Tell your mouthpiece it's the glasshouse."

I went to the phone on the wall and called the Hollywood bar. Joe was still there.

"John Milo," I said when he came on the phone. "I'm in the glasshouse."

"What's the charge?" he said.

"They haven't bothered to tell me, but I want out. And I want a lawyer."

"I'll get you one of the best," he said. "Can you pay him?"

"Sure."

"What about bail?" he asked. "You got anybody who'll go it for you?"

"Nobody I want to use. To hell with it. I got enough money to put up the bail myself if they'll release me."

"I don't know if you can be bailed out tonight. I'll try, but it might not be until morning. Where's your car?"

"I don't know. Wherever they questioned me."

"Probably Newton Street Station. I'll try to get it tonight. Otherwise, they'll haul it off to the police garage and that'll cost you more. Hold on and I'll get you out as quickly as possible."

"Okay," I said, and hung up.

A guard was waiting. He motioned me to go ahead of him. We walked down a long concrete corridor. We came to a tank cell with maybe seventy or eighty men in it. I didn't like the look of it, but we went right on by it anyway. Finally the guard unlocked a door and motioned me inside. I stepped in and almost laughed when I saw where I was.

It was also a tank, stretching the whole width of the building. There were at least sixty double-deck bunks in it. But I was the only person in it. I could guess the thinking back of it. They had decided to put me in that big empty cell all by myself with the idea that it would worry me. I couldn't have been happier. It was obviously too late to get any food, so I took off my shoes, smoked a last cigarette, and stretched out on the nearest bunk. The mattress was about as thick as a waffle; there was only one blanket and no pillow. But I was tired and I went to sleep at once.

I was awakened by music. At first I couldn't figure out

where it was coming from, but finally realized the source was somewhere in the cellblock. I glanced at my watch. It wasn't quite five o'clock. The music must be for the purpose of waking us up. I grinned and wondered what some of the old-time wardens would say about that.

I was sitting on the edge of the bed, smoking a cigarette, when the music stopped. A moment later I heard the sound of cell doors opening and then the shuffling of feet. A group of prisoners marched past my cell, probably on the way to breakfast. But no one came to unlock my door. Finally a guard came down and shoved a plate and a paper cup inside my cell.

It was my breakfast. It was a hell of a time for it and it was a hell of a breakfast. The coffee was cold and so were the powdered eggs. I was nibbling at it when the other men began marching back from their breakfast.

"Hey," one of them suddenly said, pointing at me, "how come that guy gets room service?"

Everybody laughed.

I put the rest of my breakfast near the door and lit another cigarette. About an hour later a guard came down and unlocked my door. He motioned me to come out. On the way up the corridor he let me stop and get a package of cigarettes from a machine. Then he took me down a short corridor and put me in a small cell. There were two beds in it, but again I was alone.

There isn't much to do when you're in a cell. I alternated between sitting on the bed and walking back and forth. It was about two hours before the guard came back.

"Your lawyer's here," he said, unlocking the door. He showed me which way to go, and I ended up in front of a barred window. A pleasant-looking man stood on the other side.

"John Milo?" he asked. I nodded. "I'm Harold Long. Joe Larson asked me to represent you. Is that agreeable with you?"

"Sure. First tell me what the hell I'm charged with."

"You mean the police never told you?"

"They did not, and I asked often enough."

"Well, it's five felony counts—conspiracy to receive stolen property, possession of stolen property, and three counts of burglary. Have they been treating you all right?"

"I guess so, except for not telling me what I was charged with and keeping me handcuffed for more than four hours yesterday while everyone else was walking around loose."

He frowned. "We may use that later. Do you have a record?"

"No."

"Joe said that you had some money. Will five hundred dollars be all right for my initial fee? Then we'll see what happens."

"Sure," I said. "But I can't pay you until the police release my stuff."

"That's all right. What about bail? Know anybody who will go your bail?"

"No. I have enough money for that, too, if I can get my hands on it. How much is my bail?"

"One thousand dollars. Since they're not being exactly cooperative with you, there may be a problem of getting your money for the bail. We can make something out of that later. Suppose I send a bondsman up to see you. You show him your receipt for the money they took from you and agree to give him the thousand dollars plus his fee as soon as he gets you out. Then you'll get the thousand back when it's over."

"Okay."

"I'll send a man up right away. Then I'll be here when they let you out to be sure that nothing goes wrong."

"Thanks," I said.

He smiled and left.

I turned around and the guard wasn't far away. He herded me back to my cell. This time I waited about a half hour. The guard came back and told me that a bail bondsman was there to see me. He led me to a small room. In one wall there was a grilled window, and a short, fat man was standing there. He looked tired, and I realized he probably spent all his days looking through little grilled windows.

"John Milo?" he asked.

"Yeah."

He handed a card through the window. "Harold Long said for me to come and see you. You got anybody who'll go your bail?"

"No," I said. "I don't even need anyone. I have enough money, once they release it. If you'll go my bail, the minute I'm released I'll give you the thousand dollars, plus your fee, in cash. Whenever the bail is lifted, you can give me back the thousand dollars."

"You got a receipt?"

I took it from my pocket and handed it to him. He looked at

it carefully. "All right," he said, handing it back. "I'll wait for you downstairs. Your lawyer is going to wait up here for you."

I went back to the cell and waited another half hour. Finally, still another guard came for me. He took me to the desk where I'd been printed the night before, and I signed a paper. Then I was led through another barred door and up to the desk. My attorney was standing a few feet away. He winked at me.

The cop behind the desk took his time as he got out the big manila envelope and began to remove my possessions. It took him a long time to count the money and the traveler's checks. Finally, he finished and shoved a form in front of me.

"Sign here," he said.

"One thing is missing," I said. I spoke loudly enough so my attorney could hear me.

Long moved nearer.

"What?" the cop asked.

"My gun."

"It hasn't been completely checked out yet," the cop said.

"What does that mean? You checked it to see if it was stolen, didn't you?"

"Yes."

"Well—was it?"

"No, but ..."

"No buts. It's my property and its serial number is on my permit."

The attorney moved up to the counter. "He's right, you know, officer."

"All right, all right," the cop said. He reached down and produced the gun, which he slapped on the counter.

I picked it up and looked at it. "And the bullets," I said.

He managed to produce them, too. Then I signed the paper. I took off my coat, buckled on the shoulder holster, and slipped the gun into it. I put the coat back on and placed my possessions in various pockets.

"It's been lovely," I told the cop. "Be sure to give my compliments to the chef. He must be serving time for poisoning his wife." I looked at the lawyer. "Let's go."

We went out and got in the elevator.

"The bondsman is waiting downstairs," Long said.

"I know. He told me he would be. Are you in a rush, Mr. Long?"

"No. I'm not due in court for a couple of hours. I thought I would buy you a drink. You probably need it now."

"I'll accept," I said. "I also want to talk to you as soon as I finish with the bondsman."

"All right. You don't need me while you settle with him. Do you know a restaurant called the Stake-Out?"

"Sure."

"I'll be there. I'll wait for you. The bondsman's office is only two blocks away from it."

We went downstairs and there was the bondsman. He looked the same as he had through the grilled window. I walked about four blocks with him, and we arrived at his office. I signed a paper and gave him eleven hundred and ten dollars. He gave me two receipts—one for a thousand dollars and the other for a hundred and ten.

I walked over to Main Street and went into the Stake-Out. The lawyer was sitting at the bar. I joined him.

"You have a drink coming," he said.

I asked the bartender to make me a martini. When it came, I lifted it to the lawyer.

"What about lunch?" I asked him. "I know it's early, but I could stand some decent food after that breakfast this morning. You've bought me a drink. I'll buy you a drink and a lunch."

He laughed. "I'll accept. Shall we move to a table?"

"By all means."

We picked up our drinks and picked a table next to the wall. The waitress came over and I ordered two more drinks. When she had left to get them, I pulled out some money and counted out five hundred dollars. I passed it over to Long.

"I'll mail you a receipt," he said. "Where are you staying?"

"At the Native Son Motel on Hollywood Boulevard. But you'd better send it to me in care of Joe."

"Why?"

"That's why I want to talk to you. When are we supposed to have a preliminary hearing?"

"In two days. Why?"

"I'd like it postponed. Can you do it?"

"Probably. For how long?"

"I think a month would be fine."

"Why?"

"I want to leave the country for two to four weeks. I'll come back. There is no reason why I can't leave, is there?"

"No, not if you report to me or to your bondsman and your absence is within the time of your postponement. Well, I think I can get a postponement for you on the basis of my court schedule. That's probably the easiest. But I can't get it until day after tomorrow, and you'll have to show up—I mean at the calling of the preliminary. Where are you going?"

"Hong Kong."

He whistled. "I won't ask why. Okay. We're due in 109 at nine o'clock in the morning day after tomorrow. I do have a busy court schedule starting that morning, so I think I can swing it."

"That's all I ask," I said.

We had our second drink and then lunch. Both were delicious. Then Long had a fast cup of coffee, glanced at his watch, and pushed the cup away. He took out a card and handed it to me. "That's my office number if you have to get in touch with me. Otherwise, I'll see you day after tomorrow."

"Fair enough," I said.

He left.

I ordered a second cup of coffee and some brandy. While I was having it, Joe came in. He spotted me and came over. I signaled the bartender to bring him a drink.

"How'd it go?" he asked.

"I'm out on bail," I said. "What about my car?"

"It's in the police garage. It'll cost you two bits to get it out."

"Okay," I said. I finished the coffee and brandy and paid the bill. "I'll talk to you later. Now I want a shower and some sleep."

I got up and left, and took a taxi to the police garage. I identified myself and my right to the white Cadillac, gave them twenty-five dollars, and drove it away. I went straight back to the motel, stripped off my clothes, and had a good shower and then some V.O. on ice. I finished that and went to sleep.

It was late afternoon when I woke up. I made some instant coffee and had a V.O. with it. By then I was really awake. I shaved and got dressed. Then I went out and got into the Cadillac.

I drove up to La Cienega and picked a seafood restaurant. I had three martinis and a good dinner. By the time I was finished, it was already dark. I drove back down to The Tippler and parked on a side street.

I got out of the car and headed toward the rear of the building intending to go in through the back door. But something was going on near there. Two men were talking loudly. I moved closer. The streetlight showed me both of them. I recognized them, but I knew the name of only one. He was Bob Andrews, the sick bulldog. The other was one of the men who had been taken to the police station the day before. He was a small, wizened man, probably about sixty years old. But he was carrying a pistol which was pointed at the younger man. I didn't know this guy's name. He was doing the talking as I approached them.

"I'm going to kill you," he was saying. "You're a no-good fink, and the quicker I kill you the better."

"Wait a minute," Andrews said. He sounded scared. "You got it all wrong. We're in this together."

"Hold it," I said, "both of you." I took my gun out and was holding it in my hand. "You must recognize me. You. Put the toy away. You won't solve anything that way."

He squinted at me and seemed to recognize me. Then he put the gun in his pocket.

"I guess you're right," he said, "but I can't stand a fink."

"There are better ways," I said. I walked over to them and put my gun back in the holster. "Now, what's the problem?"

"This no good bastard, Bob," the little guy said, "he's a stoolie for the cops. He's the one that got us all pinched."

"Sure," I said, "and you shoot him and then we're all in trouble. Bob, turn around and face the building."

He looked at me, still frightened.

"I put my gun away," I said. "I'm not going to shoot you. I just stopped you from being shot."

Andrews turned around and faced the brick wall.

The three of us stood like that for maybe ten seconds. "Hey," I said then, "isn't that a flying saucer up there?" Both of them looked up. I reached out and used my right hand to shove Bob's face into the wall. There was a small scream of pain from him, and when he turned around his face was a bright red. Some of it was dripping down on his shirt.

"You see," I said to the other man, "these landlubbers who call themselves sailors can't even stand without losing their balance. I'll see you around—both of you."

EIGHT

They were still standing there in the same positions, although the little guy wasn't reaching for his gun again, when I turned to enter the back door of The Tippler. I stopped in the door and looked back at the sick bulldog. The blood was still dripping down his face.

"Think how much worse it would have been if I hadn't come along," I told him. "If I were you, I'd stay away from this neighborhood for a while—starting about ten minutes ago. And be careful not to lose your balance anymore."

He nodded dumbly and started to walk toward the street, pulling out his handkerchief and beginning to mop at his face.

The little guy looked at me. "Thanks," he said. "I know you're right, but I was so damned mad I couldn't think of anything else to do. That lousy fink!"

"I know how you feel," I said. "But that way would only mean trouble for everyone. This way is better. I think he got the message, and he can't prove that he didn't stumble. It's an old cop trick, so his friends ought to appreciate the joke. I'll see you around."

"Yeah. I want to tell you something else. I don't know you, and I don't know and don't care how you got mixed up in this. But I do know eight people were pulled in and everybody talked but two. That was you and me."

"That's about par for the course. You mean the two big boys who came along at the last minute sang?"

"They only got one of the big ones—Tony Coffer. He's got a long sheet and he's got four other raps hanging over him now. That might loosen his tongue a little."

"Yeah, it's a great lubricant. I'll see you around."

I went into The Tippler. I sat down at one end of the bar by myself and ordered a drink. Word had apparently gotten around. I could tell by the way some of the customers looked at me.

"I hear you were downtown," the bartender said when he brought me my drink.

"Yeah."

"The booze deal you were talking to the boss about?"

"No. Something else I never even heard about."

"That's the way it goes sometimes, especially around here. The whole street is crawling with cops, and most of them got more ambition than brains."

I had the one drink and left. I picked up a morning newspaper and a couple of paperback books and went to the motel. I read, watched television, and had a few drinks until I got sleepy.

The next day I had breakfast near the motel. Then I phoned the airline and made a reservation for Hong Kong in the name of John Milo for the following day. There was nothing else to do until after my court appearance, so I got in the car and drove out to the beach. I had a dry martini and a seafood lunch in a restaurant where I could look at the ocean while I ate. Then I drove back to the motel in Hollywood.

I phoned the bar. Joe was there. I asked him to come down to my motel. He was there in twenty minutes. I made a drink for him and one for myself.

"I talked to Long," Joe said. "He told me you go in for the preliminary hearing tomorrow."

"Yeah. I asked him to try to get it postponed for about four weeks."

"Why?"

"I know they can't make the charge stick," I said, "but I don't want to get out of it too quickly. I want to go to Hong Kong while this is still hanging over my head. I have an airline reservation for tomorrow. If I'm able to pick it up, I'll get in touch with you. I'll give you money. I want you to go to Las Vegas, see your friend Angelo Bacci. He may know about this deal, but try in just casual conversation to let him know the bust I just got and what it involved."

"Okay."

"You can also tell him that I got a postponement so I could go to Hong Kong. But be sure that you make it casual."

"Okay."

"And don't lose all the money," I said.

"I have a feeling I'm going to win this time," he said.

"You always have the feeling and you never win. I don't care whether you win or lose, but do the work first. Okay?"

"Right, cousin."

We had a couple more drinks and then I suggested that we have dinner together.

He always liked going out to dinner, so he was all for it. He phoned his wife and told her. We finally went out and drove to the Scandia. We had a couple of drinks in the bar with the owner, then moved to the dining room. We had a wonderful Swedish dinner and then brandy and coffee. After that I took him home, and I went back to the motel. I watched some television and went to sleep.

I was up early the next morning and had breakfast in a place a block away. Then I drove down to the court and went in to meet my lawyer.

Everybody was there—except the guy who had been driving the Lincoln Continental. Even his name wasn't read off in court. There were three lawyers besides mine. Frank was there and turned out to be Frank Newton, an FBI man. As soon as the judge entered, my lawyer asked for the postponement. He read dates out of his little black book and the judge checked with the other lawyers, who also looked in their little black books. Finally, the hearing was postponed for three weeks.

My lawyer and I walked out of the courthouse. He looked at me and smiled. "Have a nice trip," he said. "I'll see you in three weeks."

I drove back up to my motel and called Big Joe. He came right down. I gave him some money and again told him what I wanted him to do. I phoned the car rental place and arranged for them to pick up the Cadillac. I packed my things, checked out of the motel, and took a taxi to International Airport.

There was only one worry when I reached Hong Kong—that was that Inspector Simmons just might happen to be there, but he wasn't. I went through customs and then got a taxi and went to the Tien Hou Hotel. It wasn't quite as nice as the Far Eastern, but it was good enough. The clerk looked at my name.

"There is a person," he said in Chinese, "who expects you and says he will see you whenever you wish."

"Tell the person that I will see him whenever and wherever it meets with his pleasure. I would like a bottle of Lor Mai Tsao and some ice in my room."

"It will be done." He clapped his hands, and a "boy"—about sixty years old—appeared to carry my luggage up to my room. Another "boy" appeared shortly thereafter with the bottle of Chinese whiskey and a bucket of ice. I had a drink while I was unpacking.

It was only a few minutes later when the clerk phoned me. "Do you know Kai Shing's club?" he asked.

"I know it."

"The person will meet you there within a half hour. You will be expected."

I thanked him and hung up. I finished my drink and left the hotel. The club was only a few blocks away, so I walked. I gave my name when I entered, and a waiter asked me to follow him. We ended up in what was obviously a private office in the rear of the building. There was already a big square bottle and two glasses on the desk. The waiter bowed and left.

I poured myself a drink and sat down. I didn't have long to wait. The door opened and Po Hing came in.

"Hi, pal," he said. "Welcome back to the mysterious East. How was San Francisco?"

"Great—what I saw of it. Your cousin Herman sent his regards."

"I'll bet he used that exact word. Herman is a square, but a smart square. Did he fix you up okay?"

"He fixed me up fine."

He sat down and poured himself a drink, tasted it, and then sighed. "I must be flipping my honorable wig."

"Why do you say that?"

He pointed a finger at me. "There you are," he said, "practically the same thing as fuzz. Here I am, a respectable river pirate, and I go out of my way to help you."

"It's my natural charm," I told him with a smile. "Besides, you're fat and bored. Where else would you find any excitement?"

"Maybe you're right, baby," he said. "Maybe I should find a new business. You want to talk or you want to listen?"

"I'll listen."

"Well, we shook up your boy a little after Herman sent that message. I saw that he got a little fuzz trouble on his last trip. He is coming back to Hong Kong tomorrow. What now?"

I thought about it a minute. Then I looked at him. There was a smile on his face.

"I get the feeling that you have a suggestion," I said.

"It depends on what you want, pal. Do you want him completely out of action? Or do you want his friends to think he's unreliable?"

"A little of both," I said. "I'd like them to think that he's unreliable and I'd also like it to be impossible for him to make the run back to the States with the money."

He looked pleased with himself. "That's the way I thought you'd want it, pal. Things have been slow on the waterfront, and I've been thinking about your problems. If you get the guy out of action, maybe you can cut back to the States and get his job, right?"

"I had something like that in mind," I admitted.

He bobbed his head happily. "Manny Keller will arrive tomorrow on a plane which lands about the time it gets dark. He will be carrying a suitcase and two sample cases. It is presumed that there will be drugs in the three containers, many of them not officially declared. Right?"

I nodded.

"Keller will be met at the airport by Larry Blake and Bernie Henderson, as he always is. This is obviously a move to give him protection so that he won't be hijacked on his way into town. Now, they escort him to a small hotel which is not far from where you are staying. Suppose they do get hijacked on the way to the hotel, but everything isn't taken because a stranger suddenly shows up and drives the hijackers away—maybe you."

"Go ahead," I said.

"Then," he said, beaming, "before they can recover and get on their way—but after the helpful stranger has already departed—the local fuzz arrives and finds a man who has illegally brought drugs into Hong Kong. Obviously such a man will be arrested and tossed into the pokey. Therefore, it is improbable that he will be able to make the return trip to the States with the loot from previous deliveries. One of the others will have to make the trip, and then it will also be obvious that other arrangements will have to be made before the next trip."

"It sounds logical," I admitted.

"So, if you have any connections back there, you jump into an early plane and are available for honorable job."

"I had something like that in mind," I said, "so stop looking as happy as a kid who has just heisted the cookie jar. How do you suggest that I arrange to do both the hijacking and the rescue? I didn't bring my Superman suit. Or are you offering me the use of your sturdy henchmen?"

"Not exactly. My men are too well known, and the whole thing would become too suspicious. But you are forgetting something."

"What?"

"The Dragon Lady of Hong Kong."

"What do you mean?"

"The men who work for her. They are not as well known to the Hong Kong police or to men such as those you are interested in. She could provide the men for the hijacking. You could then drive them away heroically. They would disappear in ways which they know; you would also vanish with certain help from me; and finally there would be left only Manny Keller and a collection of local cops."

"Maybe," I said. "I'll check with her."

"Okay, pal. But you don't have too much time. Leave word for me with the hotel clerk. Yeah, there is one other thing."

"What?"

"If the fuzz starts snooping around too much, they find that a John Milo is checked in at the Tien Hou Hotel. Inspector Simmons is not a fool, and he knows you well. The name Milo is not so common. The clerk will have instructions to notify you if Inspector Simmons wants to see John Milo. The room directly below you will be empty and you can hide in it. It may not be heroic, but it'll be safe."

"Thanks, Hing," I said. "I'll be in touch with you." He nodded and left.

I waited a few minutes, then also walked out. I stopped at a public phone booth on the way back to the hotel and called Mei Hsu. I got her at once.

"This is John Milo," I said.

"Where are you?"

"In town."

"Come up."

"Okay," I said and hung up.

I went on to the hotel and stopped to talk to the clerk. He said that he could arrange for me to rent a car and that it would be there in thirty minutes. He was as good as his word.

I drove up into the hills. The same houseboy opened the door and led the way up to Mei's apartment on the second floor. She was waiting for me in the living room. She stood until the door closed behind me and then she was in my arms.

"Ah, these scrutable Orientals," I said, when she finally stepped away from me.

"Foreign Devil," she said in Chinese, laughing as she walked across the room. "You know where the bar is. Ply the daughter of the House of Hsu with strong drink." I mixed two dry martinis and carried them over to the couch where she waited. We clinked the glasses and drank.

"How are you, Milo?" she asked then.

"All right, I think," I said. "I can't be sure when I'm around you. My blood pressure goes up, my pulse beat is faster, and there's a faint ringing of bells in my ears."

She laughed. "Those are the ancient temple bells of my country. They are supposed to carry the wisdom of generations of people. You should listen and learn."

"I always listen to the ringing of bells caused by your presence, and it disturbs me more than it educates me. But I still came back."

"So you did, Milo, but it is partly because you want something."

"You."

"More than that," she said with a smile. "You want to know what I've learned of the three men you asked me about when you were last here. Do you remember asking me?"

"Yes."

"I have not learned much, but I will tell you what I know. They are dealing with the present government on the mainland, selling them various kinds of machines and medical drugs. They are taking the money in dollars secured through a bank here in Hong Kong, which is controlled by the Communists. Presumably the money is then somehow transferred to your country. I am told that two of the Americans carry guns and are considered criminals. The two Chinese, whom you also asked me about, are known criminals and make frequent trips to the mainland. That is about all I have been able to learn. But I will continue to inquire."

"I doubt if you can learn much more than that," I said. "There is something else you can do for me—and I think it fits in with the things you are already doing."

"You see?" she said. "You do want something. What, Milo?"

"One of the three Americans brings the medical drugs into Hong Kong while posing as a legitimate salesman of drugs. He will arrive tomorrow evening with a fresh supply meant for Red China. I would like for some of your men to stop him and his two friends and take part of his shipment. I want to pretend to step in to help the others and chase your men away. I want some of the drugs left on the American so that he will be picked up by the Hong Kong police."

"It could be done," she said thoughtfully. "Is that all you want?"

"Not quite," I said honestly. "It's all as far as that one operation is concerned. But there is one additional thing I would like, if it is possible. It could tie in with your other activity. I would like to buy something which I can apparently smuggle back into the United States. It could be art objects, jewelry, or historical objects from the mainland. I will pay for them and I will pay the customs charge when I take them to the States. I will probably sell them, and if I do so for a larger price than I paid, your Hong Kong refugee fund will get the difference."

"It would have to be something that you could obtain quickly?"

"Yes. I would say something I can have within about twenty-four hours. I might need some help making it appear that I am really smuggling the objects."

She was silent for a minute. "I think there is something," she said then. "There is some *ke yu*—that is jade that was passed from generation to generation—which recently moved from the mainland to Hong Kong. It is valuable, but it is not of great historical meaning to my people. Its value is between twenty and thirty thousand American dollars, yet I doubt if it could be sold here for more than five thousand. Could you give me that much?"

"Yes."

"Then it can be arranged. As to the first thing you requested, I can give you a definite answer before this evening is over. Then you will have to let me know a place and also the time. How many men do you think will be needed?"

"I will leave that to your judgment. As I have been told, there will be three of them—all Americans. Two will undoubtedly be carrying guns. The other one will be carrying a suitcase and two drug sample cases. I am also told that there will be drugs in all three pieces of luggage. One piece, probably a sample case, should be left in the man's possession when the other men escape, after being frightened off by my shots fired at them. All of my shots will be fired over their heads."

"From where does your information come, Milo? Po Hing?"

"Yes. What made you think of him?"

"I remember that you saw him several times when you were here before, and it seemed that he might be the one you would turn to. If the information came from him, it is probably accurate. Why are you not using his men for the hijacking?"

"He said that they might be too well known."

"That is probably true. All right, Milo, darling, I will give you an answer after I make a phone call and get some arrangements made." She went to the phone, and when she returned she said, "We'll know in about an hour from now."

"Good," I said. I went over to the bar and made two more martinis and brought them back.

"Thanks, Mei."

"For you, anything. We have finished business for the time?"

"Yes."

"Wonderful. Then kiss me—properly."

I did as I was ordered. Finally, we went back to our drinks. We were on our third cocktail when her phone rang. She answered, and spoke in the dialect she had used when I had been there before. When she hung up she looked at me and nodded.

"It will be done," she said. "We can use the drugs and it will be better for them to be used here than in Peking. It is understood that we keep the drugs we take?"

"Of course. I can't ask you to return them without also admitting that I set it up."

"I will need to know the time and place and other details you have as quickly as possible."

"Then I must leave and arrange to see Po Hing at once."

"How do you do this?"

"Through the clerk at the Tien Hou Hotel."

She nodded. "The clerk is Sammy Tsing. He has long worked for Po Hing, but he once worked for my father. It might not be safe for you to phone him, although it would save much time. But perhaps I can do it for you."

"If it's unsafe for me, why will it be safer for you?"

"It is well known in Hong Kong that the Tien Hou Hotel is owned by Po Hing, and there is a possibility that the phone might be tapped. But Sammy Tsing speaks the same dialect I have been using on the phone. It is not one that many Chinese here speak, and there is no regular interpreter at the Hong Kong police who does speak it."

"All right," I said. "Make the call, but remember my name is John Milo."

She picked up the phone and put the call through. She talked in the same dialect, but the conversation was short. She replaced the receiver and turned to me. "Your desire was anticipated. Sammy Tsing said that the person you wish to speak with again is waiting for you at his home. He said that you know the location of the place and suggested that you drive there after first making certain you are not followed. If you are being followed, you should return to the hotel and other arrangements will be made."

I put down my glass. "Okay. I'll go over there right now."

"You will be back? We haven't had our dinner yet. There is a saying among my people that a man on an empty stomach is a paper dragon."

"That depends upon whose empty stomach he is on," I told her. "I'll be back," I added as she made a face.

Since I was already in the hills above Hong Kong, it took only a few minutes to drive to the house of Po Hing. I was met at the front door by the big Chinese and immediately taken to the study. As usual, Po Hing was sitting behind the desk. There was a drink in front of him.

"Greetings, pal. Help yourself to a drink."

"I'll sit this one out," I said. "The Dragon Lady's men will do the hijacking tomorrow night, but I must provide them— tonight, if possible—with every detail."

"Of course," he said with a smile. "Do you think that Po

Hing prospered this long without knowing the importance of such things? Come here."

I stepped over to the desk. He pulled a small map from a drawer in front of him and spread it out. "This is a map of the section. You will notice that I have marked several spots, although I have prudently not marked the location of the Tien Hou Hotel. It is here." He put his finger on a spot on the map. "The hotel at which Manny Keller will go is here, only six blocks away from you. He is, as I have told you, met at the airport by Blake and Henderson. They then escort him, in a black Jaguar sedan owned by Blake, to another very small hotel two blocks from where Keller will stay. Henderson and Keller will get out of the car and enter that hotel; its chief advantage is that it has entrances on two different streets. They go into one on this street and out the one on this street." His fingers indicated two markings on the map.

"What is the name of the hotel?"

"The Peking. The best place to take them is as they exit from the hotel. There will be only two of them, and it is a fairly dark street. It should be easy. Now, they normally walk the two blocks from there to the New Canton Hotel, where Keller will stay. I believe that they are met there by Ma Chok and Shan Chin, who, incidentally, just returned from the mainland today. I presume that they receive the drugs that Keller has brought and in turn give Keller the money which they have carried from the mainland. Then each goes his own way, and Keller will spend two or three days being a drug salesman."

"What about the hijacking?"

"Oh, yes. The men normally arrive at the hotel at about twenty minutes past eight o'clock. They do not make any stops, so it varies only according to the traffic. It probably takes no more than two or three minutes for them to walk through the hotel. The hijacking operation, done by skilled men, should take no more than five to seven minutes, even with the interruption which you provide."

"I wondered when we were going to get to me," I said dryly.

"Here," he said, putting a finger on another mark on the map. "There is a small tea-and-cake shop. It affords an excellent view of the exit from the hotel. You can wait there until it is time to interfere. The operator of the shop is blind. Your Chinese is good enough so that he will not be sure whether you are Chinese or a Caucasian."

"That's good."

"Here," he continued, pointing to another spot on the map, "there is a narrow alley leading to the next street. As soon as you have put the hijackers to flight, you will hurry through that alley, and at the other end you will find a car and Wing." He gestured toward the door so that I knew he was referring to the big Chinese. "He will drive you to a side entrance of the Tien Hou. In the meantime, after being rescued by you, Keller and Henderson will be continuing on their way to Keller's hotel with whatever they have managed to retain. But, most unfortunately, before they reach that destination they will be stopped by the Hong Kong police, who will discover that Mr. Keller is carrying drugs which have been brought into the port illegally. At about the time that is happening, you should be in your hotel room."

"Fine."

"One more thing, pal," he said. "There is always the possibility that someone may report to the police that a Caucasian helped to drive off the hijackers and then vanished. If so, there will be a search of the whole area. It would be well if you were prepared quickly to move to the room below the one you now occupy."

"Hing, you're a genius," I said.

"It is true," he said. "Once I saw how simple the hijacking was, I should have pulled it myself and kept the proceeds. I must be getting old."

I laughed. "Okay. Now I want to ask a couple of questions, if I may."

"Shoot, pal."

"You know how the Hong Kong police work. If Inspector Simmons happens to visit the Tien Hou Hotel and sees the name John Milo, he may get curious about the name and start checking outgoing flights."

"That is true. But unless he has more to go on, he will probably do no more than call the airport to see about reservations. Why not have a friend make a reservation and then cancel it at the approximate time you arrive there? You will then be able to get on the flight before the Inspector can find out about it and arrive there to confirm his suspicions."

"If your other guess is right," I said, "someone will probably make a reservation for a flight to the States shortly after Manny Keller is picked up by the police. Can you find out about this? And how can I reach you tomorrow night to find out—if I decide to stay somewhere other than the hotel?"

"Ah, I see," he said, nodding. "Yes, I can find out. You can have a friend call here and say that … she is calling for a brother. I will give such information as I have."

"A final question, Hing. How can I ever repay you for all you've done to help me?"

He waved a pudgy hand. "When you get back to San Francisco, buy a fortune cookie in my name."

NINE

After I left Po Hing, I drove straight back to Mei Hsu's house. I showed her the map and went over the plans and timing with her. When I'd finished, she phoned one of her men. Again they talked in the same dialect. When she had finished, she hung up and smiled at me.

"They have the plans and the time schedules," she said. "They will be there. You can depend on them, Milo."

"If you say so, I'm sure I can," I told her. "I wasn't worrying about that." While we had two more martinis I quickly sketched the rest of the picture as I saw it. She nodded in agreement with each point I made. When I had finished, she squeezed my hand and we went in to dinner. Later, we dallied over brandy and cigarettes.

It was late when I got back to the hotel. It was too late to phone down for ice, but I had a straight drink of V.O. and mulled over the plans. I had to admit that Po Hing had conceived a brilliant idea for what we wanted to accomplish. Once it succeeded, there was still going to have to be some luck, but I was certain it would not depend on luck alone.

I didn't sleep late the following morning. There was no reason to get up early, but I was beginning to be filled with the excitement that comes just before the action starts. I phoned downstairs for breakfast and some ice. I had a small drink and a leisurely breakfast. I shaved and showered and got dressed, even though I didn't have much to do during the day.

There were two things I wanted to do. First, I made the walk to the Peking Hotel and timed how long it took. I located the little tea shop, and finally walked through the alley that Po Hing had described. I returned to the hotel and found the side door. It opened easily from the outside and led directly to the elevators and the stairway.

I went up to my room and carefully cleaned and checked my gun. When I was sure it was working perfectly, I put it away. I had lunch in a small restaurant not far from the hotel. Then, for lack of anything else to do, I strolled through the shopping center and made a few small purchases. I went back to the hotel, had two drinks, and managed to take a nap.

I didn't have anything to eat before starting out for the scene of the coming action, although I did have two slow drinks. When it was time, I strapped on my shoulder holster and put the gun into it. I went down the stairs and left by the side door.

As I had planned, I reached the tea shop a little ahead of time. I went in and ordered tea and cakes from the old man behind the counter. I spoke to him in Cantonese and he answered in the same language. I paid him and carried what I had bought to a table that gave me a clear view of the street and the exit from the hotel.

It was perhaps twenty minutes before anything happened. Then two Caucasians came out of the hotel. They carried between them a suitcase and two large flat cases that looked like those used for samples. They stopped for a minute, looking around.

There was no traffic on the narrow street. As the two men stepped from the sidewalk, five figures clad in black suddenly rushed from the shadows and converged on them. I saw the flash of at least one knife, and there were two quick gunshots. I got up and went out to the street.

As I reached the sidewalk, I saw that the five men were working with admirable efficiency. They had already grabbed the suitcase and one of the sample cases. Two of them were struggling with the two Americans. I drew my gun and fired above their heads. The two Americans were immediately knocked to the ground, and the five Chinese quickly vanished back into the shadows. I fired two more shots into the air.

The two Americans were trying to get to their feet as I turned and ran down the alley, putting my gun away. There were sounds of voices from behind me, but they dwindled quickly. As I neared the end of the alley I slowed to a walk. I breathed a sigh of relief when I reached the next street. There was a car with the big Chinese sitting behind the wheel. He had the door open before I reached the car, and we were underway by the time I was in the seat. It couldn't have been more than three minutes before we stopped at the side door of the Tien Hou Hotel. I got out without saying anything to the big Chinese and went inside.

There was enough time, so I went into the lobby. It was empty except for the clerk behind the desk. I went up and put some money on the desk.

"I am not checking out," I told him. "I am merely paying for my room, including a few days in advance, and for the car which I rented but do not need in the immediate future."

"It is understood," he said, taking the money. Although he did not make it obvious, I saw that he was aware that there was a large tip included for him.

"There is one more thing," I said. "Is it possible for me to find a taxi whose driver will completely forget the call as soon as it has been completed?"

"It is possible."

"Have him at the side entrance in ten minutes. Tell him I will pay him well."

"It will be done."

I went up to my room. The first thing I did was to clean my gun and put in fresh bullets. Then I packed it in the suitcase. The spent shells were placed in some toilet tissue and rolled into a small ball and put in my pocket. I would throw it out of the cab later. Everything else was packed. I picked up the bag and went down the stairs and out the side door. There was a taxi there. I went up to the driver.

"From whom do you come?" I asked him in Cantonese.

"Sammy Tsing. He is my cousin."

I got into the cab and gave him Mei's address. He drove me there without saying another word. When we arrived, I paid him and added the same amount as a tip. Then I went inside.

Mei was waiting in the apartment. This time she had mixed the drinks.

"I have already heard," she said, "that everything went well."

"Everything?" I asked.

"I don't know about the police part of it," she said. "I mean I heard from my men. It went the way it was planned. And oh, Milo, the drugs were all things that we need very badly."

"What about one thing, honey? Is it safe to call Po Hing from here?"

"I'm sure it is."

"Call him and tell him that you are calling for a brother."

"Why a brother?"

I took the wooden ball from my pocket. "Because of this."

She looked at it, a curious expression on her face. "Where did you get it?"

"Po Hing gave it to me."

"He must like you very much. Those are never given out lightly. Do you know what it is?"

"Only what the character means. Why?"

"My father had one. It was always used as a means of identification among the members of an ancient Chinese society of thieves. It is still used for the same purpose. I will make the call for you now."

She went to the phone and dialed the number. She made the one statement in Chinese, then listened.

"*Shih,*" she said. She hung up.

"The man named Manny Keller is in the custody of the police, and they found some of the drugs on him. He doesn't have the other information yet, but will call here when he receives it."

"Are you sure this won't endanger you?"

"Quite sure," she said. She smiled. "Besides, I have an obligation to you myself now. I possess the wooden ball which was once the property of my father."

"I don't think I'll ever get used to thinking of you as my brother."

She laughed and leaned over to kiss me. We had another drink and then went in to dinner. We were just finishing coffee and brandy when the phone rang. Mei answered it and listened silently for a minute.

"Po Hing," she said, putting the receiver down. "He says that the man known as Larry Blake has booked a reservation on a plane for Los Angeles for tomorrow."

"Mei, do me one more favor," I said. "Call the airline and make a reservation for one on the earliest possible flight for Los Angeles tomorrow. Make it anytime you want, because you'll cancel it tomorrow just about the time I arrive there."

She nodded and went back to the phone. She made the reservation and came back to me. "Now," she said, "there is one more piece of business between us, Milo March. I will show you."

She went to a cabinet in one corner of the room and brought back a small box and a fairly large one. She opened the smaller one first and took out a pair of cuff links and a tie clasp.

"These three pieces of jade," she said, "are part of the collection I told you about. They've been set like this so that you can wear them when you go back. But the main part of the collection is here." She opened the larger box, and there was one of the most beautiful chess sets I had ever seen. The pieces were all carved out of jade, half in green and half in white.

"You mean that's the rest of the jade?" I asked.

"No. This chess set is a collector's item, and the pieces are jade. The set is valuable, but worth no more than perhaps twelve hundred dollars. The rest of the jade collection is concealed in the various pieces. All you have to do is remove the bottoms and take out the jade. You can then put weights in the hollow bottoms and have a beautiful chess set."

"It is that," I said.

"The purchase of the chess set was made this morning at the Chen Shop in your name, so you will have to declare it. You can be sure it will be reported."

"Okay," I said. I pulled money from my pocket and counted off five thousand dollars. "There is the money you asked for the jade. If I sell it in the States I will send you the rest of the money. Now, how much do I owe you for the chess set?"

"Nothing. It is a present from the House of Hsu."

My first instinct was to protest, but I knew that would make her unhappy, so I leaned over and kissed her. "Thanks, honey. I will always treasure it."

"We have now talked enough about business," she said firmly. "You are going away tomorrow morning and I may never see you again. I will not have the rest of the evening spoiled."

It wasn't.

The next morning Mei Hsu insisted on driving me to the airport. She said that someone else would call at the proper time to cancel the reservation she had made the evening before. She drove the car herself. It was a new Rolls-Royce, and it made me think that there were advantages to having had a father who had once been a river pirate.

When we got to the airport Mei parked and left me in the car while she went to check the terminal. She returned to report that Inspector Simmons was not there. We both walked inside, and I went up and asked about a ticket for Los Angeles on the next plane.

"You're in a spot of luck, old boy," the clerk said. "The plane was filled up, but we just had a cancellation."

I got the ticket and checked my luggage. There was about twenty minutes before flight time, so Mei and I went into the lounge and ordered drinks. We were strangely silent during the first ten minutes. Then she reached over and placed her hand on top of mine.

"Do you think you will be coming back, Milo?" she asked.

"Right away? I don't know, honey. I think I will have to, but there's no way of knowing at the moment."

"I realize that," she said. "But you won't just vanish and never come back, will you?"

"Not if I can help it."

"If you try, I'll come after you," she said firmly.

"I hope that's a promise." I tore a sheet of paper out of an address book and wrote down my New York addresses and phone numbers and handed it to her.

"The first is my office and the second is my apartment. If I'm out of town, my answering service will tell you when I should be back. If you're really a wily Oriental, you might get them to tell you where I am."

"Thanks, Milo," she whispered.

Then it was time for my flight. She walked with me to the gate. She lifted her head to kiss me. "Good luck, Milo," she said.

When the plane was lumbering down the runway, I could see her standing on the observation deck. She waved and I waved back, even though I didn't think she could see me.

I didn't know what Larry Blake looked like, but I was pretty sure he wasn't on this plane. When I'd been given a seat number, I'd seen the other names on the list and his hadn't been there. So maybe I had a few hours of extra time.

When we reached Los Angeles, I went through customs. I declared the chess set and paid the duty on it. They didn't think of looking inside the pieces, and no attention was paid to the cuff links and tie clasp I was wearing. Then I caught the next flight to Las Vegas. There, I took a cab to the Sultan's Palace. That was the hotel where Big Joe had stayed, and it was also owned by Angelo Bacci. I was already gambling without ever going near a table.

TEN

I checked into the hotel and asked the clerk to order a rented Cadillac for me. I went up to the room and called room service to order a bottle of V.O. and some ice. Then I unpacked and called the valet service for some rush laundry and dry cleaning. A waiter arrived fairly soon with the ice and the booze. I signed the check and gave him a big tip. Another man arrived from the valet service to pick up my clothes. I also gave him a big tip. I figured it was the best way to make sure that Angelo Bacci discovered I was in the hotel.

After making a drink, I took out the chess pieces and went to work on them. They were so beautiful that I hated to tamper with them at all. But I soon discovered it was not too difficult to remove the bottom of each piece. A few minutes later I had quite a collection of jade on the bed. There was a necklace, several rings, and a number of pieces carved in the form of birds and animals. They were all beautiful.

The phone rang. It was the desk. My Cadillac had arrived.

I wrapped all of the jade, including the cuff links and the tie clasp, in a handkerchief and put it in the pocket of my jacket. Then I buckled on my shoulder holster and slipped the gun into it. I put on the jacket and was ready to go downstairs. The clerk gave me the name of the biggest and most expensive jeweler in town. I went out, got into the car, and drove down to the shopping center.

It wasn't hard to find the jewelry store. Inside, I asked to see the owner or the manager. A distinguished-looking man appeared from the back and asked what he could do for me.

"I have what may be an unusual request," I said. "I have some jade which is quite old. I would like you to examine it and give me an appraisal of its value, item by item, and I would like the appraisal notarized. Naturally, I'm willing to pay for it."

"It may take a few hours," he told me.

"That's all right," I said. I took the folded handkerchief from my pocket and put it on the counter. "I'd like one additional thing, which I will also pay for. I would like a photograph made of each piece, and I want two copies of each photograph."

"We will need about five hours."

"That's all right," I said. "I'm staying at the Sultan's Palace, but I would prefer returning here, if you would tell me a time."

"I think we can do that, Mr. ... ?"

"Milo. John Milo."

He went into the back of the store and returned with a partially printed form. He carefully noted on the form each piece of jade and the purpose for which it was left. I checked it over when he had finished and it looked all right. I signed it and he signed it. I left the jade with him and went out, stopping at one of the downtown gambling casinos to use a public phone and call Big Joe Larson.

"Hi, cousin," he said when he came on the phone. "You back already?"

"Yeah. I'm in Vegas. Did you have that talk with your friend up here?"

"Sure. He was interested and he seemed to know about the bust, but he didn't tip anything."

"Good. Now, I want you to do something for me."

"Anything."

"I'm going to telegraph you some money. It should be there in about an hour, so wait for it. Got a paper and pencil?"

He told me to wait a minute. When he came back I told him the list of things I wanted him to buy and where to get them.

"As soon as you have it all," I said, "catch the first plane to Las Vegas. When you arrive, check the package in my name. Walk out into the airport parking lot and look for a black Cadillac, a new one, with the radio running even though there's no one in it. Reach up and tape the reclaim ticket to the top of the car. Then catch the next plane back to Los Angeles."

"No dice?" he asked wistfully.

"Not this time, Joe. I don't want anyone to get the idea that you and I are working together. I'll send the money right away. It should be there in an hour. Giving it a little leeway, you should be able to buy everything and get here with it in four hours. Right?"

"Sounds like it."

"Okay. I'll talk to you later."

I hung up and went out to find the nearest Western Union office, where I wired a thousand dollars to Joe, and then drove back to the Sultan's Palace. I went in and played at the dice table for a while, winning one minute and losing the next, but I didn't see Bacci. I wandered into the bar and had a couple of drinks, then went up to my room. I rested for a couple of hours before going down to drive out to the airport. I parked the Cadillac, left the radio on, and went into the bar.

I was on my second or third drink when I heard them announce a flight from Los Angeles that sounded like it might be the right one. I moved to a spot where I could see the passengers come in through the terminal. Sure enough, there was Big Joe hurrying along to the checkroom with a bulky package. Then he bustled out and headed for the parking lot. I settled my tab at the bar and went outside. Joe was already on his way back to the terminal. He passed me without showing any sign of recognition.

When I reached the car I felt along the roof, then ripped the tape away. There were a few other cars around, but no one was paying any attention to me. I went back to the terminal and claimed the package Joe had brought.

As I left, I caught a glimpse of Joe having a drink in the bar. I put the package in the trunk of the car and drove back to the city, down to the shopping center, and parked in the reserved area in back of the jewelry store.

I went inside and they had the appraisal and photographs ready for me. The photographs were fine; so was the appraisal, which valued the jade at $25,000. I paid them for their work.

"Mr. Milo," the man said, "you realize that this appraisal is based on the retail value of the jade. But if you'd care to sell the pieces right now, we are prepared to offer you twenty thousand dollars."

"I might come back and take you up on it later," I told him. "In the meantime, thanks."

He nodded, and I went back to the car.

There was no one else in the parking area, so I opened the trunk of the car. The package contained things I might not need right away, but I removed the tape recorder and fixed it in one section of the trunk. It would be activated by the sound of a voice, or any other sound, broadcast over a special transistor microphone located anywhere within five hundred yards of the recorder. I removed two such microphones from the package and then locked the trunk.

I drove straight back to the hotel and turned the car over to a boy to park it in the hotel garage. Then I went up to my room. The first thing I did was to make a drink for myself. Fortunately, there was still some ice left. I sat, sipping the drink and looking around the room. Finally, I hit on what I thought was the simplest idea. I had one new shirt in my luggage, which meant I had pins. I pinned the jade into the handkerchief and then pinned the whole thing to the other side of the draperies. I stepped back to admire my handiwork. It was good. The draperies were heavy enough so that nothing showed.

I went back to my drink. While I was sipping it, I picked up the phone and made a reservation for one for dinner. I poured another drink and looked at my two microphones. One was in a tie clasp and the other was a wafer-thin disk that could be carried in a pocket or dropped anywhere and escape notice. Both had an on-off switch. They were off at the moment. I put them on the night table and finished my drink.

I undressed, took a shower, and shaved. Then I got dressed again, put the tie clasp on my tie, and put the other microphone in my pocket. I put on the holster and gun, and slipped on my jacket. I went downstairs to the bar and ordered a martini. I had just started to drink it when Angelo Bacci showed up.

"Hello, there," he said. "I just saw your name on the reservation list for dinner. I didn't know you were back in town."

"I just got back," I said. "Have a drink."

"Not now, thanks. Maybe I'll have one with you at dinner. How was Hong Kong?"

"It was fine," I said.

"Back on business or pleasure?"

"Mostly on business, but I may have a little pleasure. It all depends."

"Okay," he said lightly. "Glad to see you back, John. I'll talk to you later." He drifted away.

I smiled to myself and went back to my martini. Then I checked my gun with the guy at the door of the gambling room and tried the dice table. I won a couple hundred dollars and then went in to dinner. I was led to one of the best tables. I ordered a martini. The waiter came back with two martinis.

"On the house," he said.

At about the same time, Angelo Bacci showed up at my table. "Mind if I join you for a minute?" he asked.

"Why should I? It's your hotel. You're paying for the drinks, and there are two of them. Sit down."

He pulled up a chair. "How come I haven't heard of you?" he asked.

"I don't have a press agent," I said.

He smiled. "I did hear that you got into a beef in Los Angeles only a few days ago."

"Why should you hear about that? It was a small rap and a bum one. And I'll beat it."

"You got a postponement. How come?"

"You ask a lot of questions. I had business to take care of."

"In Hong Kong?"

"In Hong Kong."

"Now the same business brings you back here?"

"Maybe. Maybe it'll take me on to another place. What about it?"

"That's what bothers me. I usually know about guys like you. Some of them are punks. You're not. That means I should know about you."

"I'm allergic to being known about."

"Okay. You got a record?"

"No."

"What are you doing here? Buying or selling?"

"Selling."

"Hot?"

"Not in the sense you mean," I said. "Are you a buyer or just being nosy?"

"I might be a buyer or steer you to one. What's the merchandise?"

"Jade."

He looked at me. "It could figure. From Hong Kong?"

I smiled at him. "From Red China. You think they're going to yell for cops?"

"Old jade?"

"Old. It is the jade that is known as *ke yu,* which means it was handed down from generation to generation."

"What have you got?"

"Are you a buyer?"

"I might be," he said.

"I'm not going to show you anything here."

He glanced at his watch. "I have a business associate coming to see me soon. How about showing me the merchandise up in my suite right now?"

I shook my head. "I'll show you photographs and an appraisal from a Las Vegas jeweler. If you like what you see and we agree on a price, you can see the real things tomorrow—after you've checked with the jeweler—and give me cash for them."

He stared at me for a moment. "Suite A in five minutes," he said.

He pushed his glass away and got up and left. I smiled to myself and finished my martini. Then I beckoned the waiter and asked him to hold the table until I got back. I gave him ten bucks to make sure he remembered.

I went upstairs and got the photographs and the appraisal from the jewelry store. Then I took the elevator up to the penthouse level and went to Suite A. Bacci answered the door. He looked at me sharply.

"You're still wearing a piece," he said. "Why? You think I'm going to pull something?"

"No. But I never liked to take a bath with my socks on, and I never liked to be caught out in the rain without my rubbers on."

He laughed. "Come on in. Like something to drink?"

"Not now. This is business. I'll drink when I go back down to the dining room."

"Okay. What do you have?"

It was a nice apartment. I sat down in one of the chairs and produced the pictures.

He looked them over. "They look pretty," he said. "So what?"

I handed him the appraisal. He went over to a fancy-looking desk against one wall and began checking the appraisal against the pictures. While he was doing that, I slipped the thin microphone down beside the seat of the chair and switched both microphones on. When he finished looking, he came over and sat opposite me. "What's the story?" he asked.

"I told you," I said. "The stuff came out of Red China. It's all good jade, and you can see what the local jewelry store thinks of it. Maybe somebody stole it from Red China, but no one did any stealing after that. I bought it in Hong Kong and brought it here. I'm offering it for sale."

"When can I see the jade itself?"

"If you're interested, and we can agree, you can see it tomorrow. We'll go together with the jade to the store, and you can verify everything. I presume you know the store?"

He smiled. "I ought to. It's owned by my brother-in-law."

"Then you got no worries."

"Maybe. You brought it here from Hong Kong?"

"I said so."

"Through customs?"

"I said I brought it here. I didn't say how or in what way."

His smile got more wolfish. "You mean you didn't pay customs duties on it?"

"I didn't say that either. But I'll give you a bill of sale to Angelo Bacci from John Milo. What more do you want? Blood?"

"I'm interested," he said, "because there's a broad I want to give something special to. Something from Angelo Bacci that she couldn't get anywhere else. You understand. I'll give you fifteen grand for the lot—if they stand up when I see them."

I laughed. "I like you and you're a good friend of Big Joe's, but you must be kidding. The store will pay me more than that."

"They won't if I tell them not to."

I shrugged. "So there are a lot of other stores and collectors in the country. I didn't make a pitch to you."

It was his turn to laugh. "I like you, John. You're a gutsy guy and there aren't too many of them around anymore. How much did the store offer you?"

"Twenty."

"Okay. We can check that tomorrow. If it's true, I'll give you twenty-one, but we don't haggle after that. Okay?"

"Okay."

"Can I keep the pictures?"

"Sure." I had other copies, so it was all right.

"Okay. We'll get together tomorrow."

I nodded and left. I went downstairs and had my dinner, and watched part of the show, but then I got bored and left. As I went through the bar on my way to the gambling rooms, I saw Angelo Bacci sitting there with a tall blond guy. I wouldn't have paid any attention except that the guy got a startled expression on his face when he saw me, and then started talking to Bacci. I pretended to not notice and went on into the gambling room. I bought some chips and started at the dice table. A few minutes later I saw Bacci and his friend go to the elevators.

I played for three or four hours and ended up winning a grand total of something like fifty dollars. I cashed in the chips and went to the bar for another hour. Finally I went upstairs.

I checked the draperies and the jade was still safe. Then I called room service for ice and had a nightcap or two while I watched television.

I was up early the following morning, had breakfast in my room, and then went down, got into the car, and drove out into the desert. I found a good lonely spot and stopped. I unlocked the trunk and set the tape recorder on rewind. When it was back in its original position, I put it on play and pressed the button.

The first part was my conversation with Bacci. It was loud and clear—all of it good. Then the next sound was that of the door opening and closing.

"Want a drink?" It was Bacci's voice.

"Yeah. Bourbon, if you got it."

"I've got everything," Bacci said. There was a strong note of arrogance in his voice. Then there was the sound of glass against glass, ice cubes against glass, and the pouring.

"Now, tell me what happened," Bacci said.

"We got hijacked," the other voice said. "Bernie and Manny

go through the Peking Hotel as always and they no more than hit the street when five Chinks jump them. Two of them are punching at Bernie and Manny while the other three are trying to grab the cases. They fired a couple of shots and one guy was waving a knife. Bernie never had a chance to pull his gun. Then, suddenly, out of nowhere, this other guy shows up and starts shooting at the Chinks. Boy, they took off like someone had tied firecrackers to their tails. No sooner are they running than the other guy ducks down an alley and disappears. Bernie and Manny start walking fast for the hotel. But they don't make no more than a block when the cops move in. Bernie takes off fast, but they grab Manny with the one remaining case of drugs. The cops must've been right around the corner when they heard the shots. They got there that fast. Anyway, Manny's in the cooler. And it don't look good."

"And this man who came to the help of Bernie and Manny, you say, was John Milo, the man you saw downstairs?"

"Yeah. He's the one all right. I was just going across the intersection a half block away and I saw the whole thing. It was over before I could stop the car and help them. But that's the guy. I got a real good look at him when he ducked into the alley getting away."

"Ever see him before, Larry?"

"No, Mr. Bacci, but he's the guy all right."

"Did Bernie or Manny know him?"

"They say they never saw him before."

"Interesting. Why do you think he came to help them?"

"The way we figured it, he was a guy who saw five Chinks jump two white guys and stepped in. There was a little tea joint right near there, and he came out of it. He must've seen the action through the window."

"Yeah. You got a mouthpiece for Manny?"

"Bernie's getting him—one of the best. But it don't look too good for Manny. That's the reason we figured I'd better catch a plane and bring back the money and the news."

"That was good thinking, Larry. You stopped off in L.A.?"

"Yeah. I thought I'd better. I went down to Five Brothers Drug and told them to hold off on receiving shipments until we know whether there's a leak or not. Maybe you'd better tell them in Arizona, too."

"Maybe. The important thing is to find out who did the hijacking. Any ideas?"

"No, but that don't mean nothing. Hong Kong is full of gangs all stealing from each other. They probably just noticed Manny's regular trips and figured he must've been carrying something. Or maybe there was some kind of leak from the China side."

"What about the two local boys you're using?"

"They never had it so good. I don't think they could get enough to pay for a double-cross. But we got to get a new bagman."

"I don't know of anybody that's free right now. But there is another possibility. I'll know more about it tomorrow."

"What's that?"

"This John Milo. The one who helped Bernie and Manny get away. He looks like a good guy. He likes a buck, but he ain't starving. He's a loner, but we might get him, and he's apparently set up a pattern of going in and out of Hong Kong."

"Whatever you say, Mr. Bacci."

"We'll see what happens tomorrow. He's trying to sell me something. If it checks out, maybe we can use him."

"Okay."

"Stick around until tomorrow. Then we'll see."

"Okay. See you later, Mr. Bacci."

The next sound was the opening and closing of the door. Then there was nothing.

I rewound the tape, took off the reel, and put on a fresh one. I locked the trunk and drove back to the hotel. There was a message for me at the desk. It said that Mr. Bacci was in the grill and would like me to join him. So I did.

"Where were you?" he asked between bites of ham and eggs.

"Out," I said. I ordered a martini from the waitress. "I like to go out and drive in the desert early in the morning. I'm a nature lover."

"Yeah? Then why the martini? You drink too much."

"There are two things that you cannot have too much of. One of them is drink."

He laughed. "Okay. What about the jade?"

"Anytime you want to go."

"As soon as I finish breakfast."

"I'll get the pieces," I said.

I finished the martini and went upstairs. I unpinned the handkerchief and stuck it in my pocket. Then I went back. I stopped at the desk and told the clerk to have a boy bring my car up to the front.

Bacci had just finished his coffee. "Let's go," he said. "I'll tell them to send my car up."

"Mine is already out front," I told him.

He gave me a sharp look, but didn't say anything. We went outside.

The boy was just delivering my Cadillac. We got into it and drove down to the jewelry store. This time when the manager came out he got very humble as soon as he saw Bacci. I brought out the jade. Bacci compared it with the photographs and had the manager verify they were the pieces that had been appraised.

"Okay," he said to me. "You'll give me a bill of sale?"

"Sure."

"Make it up," he said to the manager.

"In duplicate," I added.

The manager scurried away, and we waited. He came back with the bill of sale. I signed it, turned the jade over to Bacci, and he counted out $21,000. Mei's refugees were going to do a little better than they had expected.

We drove back to the hotel. "Thanks, John," Bacci said when we got out of the car. "You going to be around for a while?"

"Probably only a day or two. I've made my sale. Now I have to look for something else to sell."

"I'll talk to you later," he said. "I might have something that will interest you."

"I'll listen," I told him.

He disappeared somewhere inside the hotel, and I stopped to play a slot machine for a few minutes. Then I moved on to the dice table and played for a couple of hours. After that I retired to the bar to lick my wounds. I recovered after two martinis and went to the grill for lunch.

After lunch I want back to the dice table. This time my luck was a little better. I was in the middle of a nice little winning streak when one of the housemen came up and asked if I was Mr. Milo. When I said I was, he said that Mr. Bacci wanted to know if I would come up to his suite. I sighed and gave up the dice.

Bacci opened the door and let me in. "How about a drink this time?" he asked.

"Okay. V.O. on the rocks will be fine."

He went over to a small bar and poured the drink. He gave himself a bourbon on the rocks. He handed me my drink, and then went to sit in a chair across the room.

"You go to Hong Kong often?" he asked.

"Only when I have some business there," I said.

"Ever have any trouble with the cops there?"

"No."

"I hear that you got into a little shooting affair in Hong Kong the last trip."

I pretended to be surprised. "How'd you hear that?"

He smiled. "I get information. How'd you get mixed up in that?"

"Just happened to see a bunch of Chinks jump two guys who looked like they were Americans. Or British. I scared the Chinks off, and that's all there was to it."

"I heard that you took off as soon as it was over. How come you didn't stick around to meet the two guys?"

"Why should I? I helped them out of a jam, but that didn't mean that I wanted to become buddies. All that noise was bound to attract some cops, and I didn't feel like enlarging my circle of friends."

"You're right about one thing. The cops picked up the two guys within a block or so from where you saw them."

"It seems to me," I said, "that you have a lot of information for a man who's sitting around in a plush hotel this far from Hong Kong."

"I ought to have. Those two guys work for us."

"Us?"

"The organization. Don't pretend to be stupid, Milo. Big Joe would have told you if you weren't able to guess. The point is, do you want to work for us?"

"I don't know," I said. "I've always liked working for myself."

"You can still do jobs on your own—as long as you don't step on any of our toes."

"That's a lot of toes not to step on."

He smiled, but without humor. "It leaves a lot of work you can do. You can always bring stuff out like this last time."

"Maybe. You haven't said what the job is yet."

"Carrying medicine to Hong Kong and bringing back money."

"That's all?" I asked. "You could get anybody to do that. Why me?"

He shook his head. "Not anybody. The medicine is stuff like antibiotics, and it's hot. You'll have a cover job as a drug salesman selling legitimate drugs. But it's the hot stuff that has to go through. And you'll be bringing money back. Lots of it in cash, and it has to get through. So not just anybody. It has to be a guy who's smart and who can be tough when he has to be."

"What happened to the boy who must have been doing it for you until now?"

"Somewhere along the line he must not have been smart enough," he said coldly. "He was one of the two men you helped in Hong Kong. Most of the stuff he was carrying was stolen by the five Chinks. But he still had enough left to spell trouble when the cops stopped him. It all adds up to the fact that he stopped being smart."

"It figures," I admitted.

"Let me hear how you figure it," he said.

"How long was he running this little errand?"

"A year. Before that he was a bagman for some very important people—and for years."

"Then somebody must have set him up," I said. "Twice. Once with the hijackers and once with the cops."

"Yeah," he said. "Somebody certainly set him up with the hijackers. Maybe he even set himself up. It's been known to happen. I guess it's possible that the cops just happened to be near and heard the shooting, and got there in time to catch my boy. But I don't believe it. I think somebody called the cops and suggested they be around the neighborhood. This brings up several angles. Got any ideas on that?"

"I could make a few," I said. "Let's look at the hijacking first. If you're taking hot stuff into Hong Kong, you must be selling it in Red China. Hong Kong is full of gangs who also make money by dealing with the mainland. Some of them also have organizations—even older than yours. I would guess that one of those gangs set up the hijacking. They probably got enough of a haul to give them a nice profit."

"And the cops?"

"How the hell do I know? Maybe the hijackers set it up so that your boy would be out of action in case he recognized anybody. So then I walk into them."

"That's why I'm offering you the job. I figure you can handle it."

"There are two little answers you haven't given me yet."

"What?"

"What about your cover? If the cops have your man, then his drug front is blown."

He nodded. "We'll have a new cover for you within two days. What's the other answer?"

"Nothing's been said about money. It's a subject about which I feel very tender."

"I told you that you can do jobs on your own as long as it doesn't interfere. You'll actually have to work for us only four or five days every three weeks, but we'll give you a grand a week. That's for every week."

"When do you want me to start?"

"The pay starts the minute you say yes. Your first trip will probably be in four or five days, depending on when a delivery is made."

"Okay. I'll try it out for size. I'll keep in touch."

"Going somewhere?"

"Yes. I live in San Francisco. I'll go there and check on everything. Then I'll run down to L.A. and check in with my lawyer. There's some unfinished business there. I'll call you every day if you want me to, but you can reach me in San Francisco at the Bay Palace Hotel or in Los Angeles at the Native Son Motel."

"All right. But call me every night anyway."

"I will," I said. I turned and walked to the door.

"One thing, John Milo," he said, "we forgot as a possibility about Hong Kong. There was somebody else who might have set up the hijacking and arranged for the cops to be there at the right time."

I turned. "Who?"

"You," he said softly.

ELEVEN

There was a conversation stopper if I ever heard one. I pulled my hand away from the doorknob as though the metal had suddenly become hot and turned to look at him. He was still sitting in the same position, the same humorless smile on his face.

"What's the gag?" I asked.

"No gag. But it could have been you. You were in Hong Kong. You're a smart operator. You were on a job where you might have gotten information about the drug delivery. You were conveniently in the neighborhood and chased the hijackers off after they got most of the drugs."

"It's a nice theory," I said. "It's a kind of job I suppose I might have pulled, if I had known about it and if I didn't like to work alone. And what's your explanation about the cops?"

"Well, it did get rid of our man who was making the deliveries. And you showed up here right afterwards, and now you have the job of making the deliveries."

"Not if that's what you think about me," I said. "We can forget the whole thing right now. I didn't ask you for a job, and you can easily get yourself another boy."

"Take it easy," he said. "I didn't say I thought you did it. The possibility occurred to me—that's all. I want you working for me." He grinned suddenly. "If there is anything to the possibility, you'll be where I can find out what you're doing."

"I thought that's what you were going to say," I told him. "I'll keep in touch."

I opened the door and went out.

I stopped at the bar downstairs and had a martini. Then I phoned and made a reservation on a plane for San Francisco. I paid my hotel bill and told them I was checking out. I gave the hotel in San Francisco as a forwarding address, paid for the Cadillac, and arranged to leave it at the airport. Then it was time to go upstairs and pack. I had a boy take my luggage down and leave it there until I was ready to go. I had another drink at the bar, took another turn at the dice table, and then it was time.

Driving to the airport, I stopped at a little store and bought another suitcase. The store had parking spaces in the rear. I quickly packed the tape recorder and the other equipment in the suitcase and got rid of the box in which Joe had brought them. Then I went on to the airport.

When I reached San Francisco, I went straight to the hotel and up to my room. The bottle of V.O. was still there, so I called down for some ice. I waited until it was delivered and I had a drink. I needed it. Then I took the tape recorder out of the suitcase and played what I had. My conversation with Bacci was on the new tape, and there was another conversation between Bacci and Larry Blake that gave me some more on the Hong Kong operation. I packed the machine away again.

I went to Herman Po's for dinner, where I ordered a drink and told the waiter I would be honored if Mr. Po would join me.

Herman came out in about ten minutes. I ordered drinks for both of us.

"You look," he said, when the drinks had been served, "like a man who wants more than dinner."

"I do. I want to know where I can charter a small plane with a pilot—one who won't ask too many questions and who will keep his mouth shut."

"For how long a trip?"

"To Phoenix, Arizona, and back. I might want to stay over there one night."

"When do you want to leave?"

"I'm not sure. Either tonight or early in the morning."

He nodded his head. "It can be arranged. But if it's to be tonight, I should know as soon as possible. You can make the financial arrangements with the pilot when you meet him."

"I'll call you soon after I leave here." I said.

He nodded again and left me.

After dinner I went back to my hotel. I got some change and went into a public phone booth in the lobby. I placed a person-to-person call to Angelo Bacci. I didn't have to wait long.

"Where are you calling from?" he asked.

"A phone booth in the lobby of my hotel. And I'm using quarters so it won't appear on my bill."

"Smart boy. It's a good thing you called. There's been a change of plans. You're not going overseas."

"Why?"

"We're going to send a dummy in for the first trip to see if anyone is waiting for him. If they are, he won't have anything. But you'll get paid for going somewhere else."

"Where?"

"I want you to go to L.A. tonight. But unless you have to, don't take a regular flight. See if you can grab a small charter plane and go to Burbank instead of International. Call me back as soon as you find out and let me know where you'll arrive and at about what time. I'll give you the rest then."

"Okay." I hung up and waited until the operator rang to tell me how much more I owed. Then I phoned Herman Po.

"There's been a slight change. I want the plane for tonight for Burbank Airport in L.A. And he won't have to bring me back."

"All right. Be at the airport here in two hours. The plane will be chartered in the name of Mr. Hing. Just announce yourself at the information desk. The pilot will be waiting there. He will be a young Chinese. Show him the wooden ball you carry."

"Thanks, Herman," I said.

I hung up and went into the hotel bar. I didn't want to call Bacci too quickly; he might think it strange I could get a charter flight within a few minutes. I had a couple of leisurely drinks, then went back to the phone booth. Bacci came on the phone right away.

"What's the story?" he asked.

"I've got a charter to Burbank. Leaving from here in an hour and a half."

"Good. Arrange to have a rental car waiting for you when you get there. And not a fancy Cadillac like you get when you're here. Something that won't attract so much attention. You'll be met at Burbank."

"How will I recognize the guy meeting me?"

"You'll know him and he'll know you. His name is Tony Coffer, and you were in court with him. He'll transfer some things to your rented car. You're to drive to Phoenix, Arizona, and check into the Cactus Palace Hotel. Someone else will come to see you there. He'll identify himself by saying Angelo sent him. He'll tell you what to do next."

"Okay. You want me to drive straight through tonight?"

"No. It's better in daylight. Check in at your regular place in L.A. Then I suggest you drive until you're past most of the worst traffic sections, stay in a motel, and start early in the morning. That will get you to Phoenix in plenty of time."

"That's all?"

"That's about it. When you're finished, return to L.A. and wait until you hear from me. What was the name of the place? The Native Son Motel?"

"Right."

He hung up without saying anything more. I went upstairs and packed. There didn't seem to be much point in packing the tape recorder I had used, so I decided to leave it. I went downstairs and told the clerk I would be away for a few days. I sent off a telegram to Los Angeles arranging for the car. Then I took a taxi to the airport.

I was there a little early, so I went into the lounge for a drink. Then I went to the information desk and said that I was Mr. Hing and would they know where I'd find my charter plane. Before they could answer, a young Chinese stepped smartly up beside me.

"Mr. Hing?" he asked.

"Yes," I said. As I turned to him I had the wooden ball in my hand.

"Let me help you with your luggage, sir," he said. "I'll show you how to reach my plane."

I followed him to a gate at the end of the terminal. He identified himself to a man there and we went through. Nothing more was said until we reached his small plane, which was not far away. There we settled the matter of money and climbed into the plane.

He started the motors and got in touch with the tower. We had to wait about five minutes before he was told to take off.

"If you look beside you on the seat," he said, once we were in the air, "you will find a bottle of Chinese whiskey. Mr. Po said that you were very fond of it."

He was right. There was a bottle there. I took a swig out of it. "May your ancestors," I said in Cantonese, "always be proud of you."

"Sorry, sir," he said with a smile. "I don't speak the language."

I laughed. "Oh, well, we can't have everything. I'm grateful for the bottle."

"Mr. Po was sure you would be. He said it is very dull to fly in a small plane with no drinks and no pretty stewardesses."

"Mr. Po is a philosopher," I said gravely.

I don't especially like small planes, or even large ones, but the trip was faster and more pleasant than I had expected. Before I realized it, he was talking to the Burbank tower, and shortly thereafter we were going in for a landing.

"Are you going right back?" I asked him.

"Yes, but first I will help you with your luggage."

"I can manage it," I said. "Thanks for the flight. It was real groovy."

"I speak that language," he said with a smile.

I took my luggage and trudged over to the terminal. I headed directly for the car rental desk. On the way I saw Tony Coffer but paid no attention to him, and he paid none to me. I identified myself at the desk, and we went through the formula of renting the car. They were a little unhappy because I didn't want to use a credit card but insisted on making the deposit in cash. I gave them a Los Angeles address as well as the San Francisco one, and told them I'd probably use the car for three or four days. They offered to bring the car around to the front, but I told them I'd be glad to go get it if they'd tell me where it was. They did so—reluctantly.

I found the car out in the parking lot without too much trouble. I unlocked the trunk and left it open. Moving slowly, I started to put my luggage in the back of the car. Just then another car pulled into the parking space next to mine. Tony Coffer was in it. He got out without saying anything and looked around. Then he unlocked the trunk of his car and swiftly transferred several large cases to the trunk of my car. He slammed it shut and did the same to his. By that time I had my luggage put away.

"Good luck," he said. He got into his car and drove away.

I crossed over the pass and took the Hollywood Freeway, getting off at Vermont. I drove to my L.A. motel and went in and registered. I didn't waste much time in the motel, just enough to check a map to make sure of my route to Phoenix. Then I went out and headed east.

When I'd finally driven far enough to be sure I'd miss most of the early morning traffic, I started looking for a motel. I finally found a deluxe one, complete with restaurant and cocktail lounge. I stopped and registered. I carried my luggage into the room and then went to the cocktail lounge. I ordered a drink, had a couple of sips from it, and went to a public phone. I called the bar in Hollywood and asked if Big Joe was there. He was.

"I'm on my way to Phoenix," I told him. "You know anyone there who can dig up some information for me? Accurate and fast."

"I know just the man," he said. "His name is Henry Gage. A private detective. Tell him you're a friend of mine."

"Thanks, Joe. I'll probably be back tomorrow night and I'll call you." I hung up and went back to my drink. Later I called it a day and left an early call with the office.

I was up by daylight, had a quick breakfast, and was on my way. I made a couple of short stops during the trip, but I was hot and tired by the time I finally arrived in Phoenix. I found the hotel and checked in. I still had part of a bottle of V.O. in my suitcase, so I had them send up some ice. I had a drink, then stripped off my clothes and had a good hot shower. I had barely gotten dressed when there was a knock on the door. I opened it and saw a little swarthy guy standing there. He looked like a movie version of a thug.

"John Milo?" he asked.

"Yeah."

"Angelo sent me." He came into the room and I shut the door. "You're late."

"I am like hell," I said. "I followed the instructions exactly as they were given to me."

"Well," he said, "maybe they didn't know the exact flight time. But the plane is practically loaded and is supposed to take off any minute. Where's the stuff?"

"In my car."

"Well, it was supposed to be handled different, but I guess you better drive it to the plane. I'll go with you. Let's get moving."

I shrugged into a jacket and we went out.

We got into the car and he gave me directions. We finally came to what was obviously a private landing field. There were several large buildings inside the fence, including several hangars. A sign on one building identified it as the Naples Air Express. There was a plane in front of one of the hangars, and there were some men still loading large cartons into it.

We came to a stop in front of a gate. My companion leaned out and waved to the guard, who opened it. "Drive right up to the plane," the man with me said. I drove across the field and stopped beside the plane. "You wait here," he said. "Give me the key to the trunk."

I turned off the ignition and handed him the key. He got out and motioned to a couple of men as he went around to the rear of the car. I sat and watched them take the cases out of the trunk and put them in the plane. The little guy came back and gave me the keys.

"Okay, pal," he said. "You've done your job. I'm staying here. You can head back to L.A."

"Not until I've had some sleep, pal," I said. "And something to eat."

"Okay. But take off." He slammed the car door shut and I drove away.

The guard opened the gate and I turned in what I thought was the general direction of the hotel. I checked behind me, but there didn't seem to be anyone following me. After a few hits and misses I found the hotel again. I parked the car in the basement garage and went back to my room.

The ice hadn't melted, so I fixed myself a drink and sat down to think about it. By the time I had finished the drink, I had a couple of ideas—for whatever they were worth. First I picked up a phone book and found a number for Henry Gage, Private Detective. I asked the hotel operator to get me the number. I went through another operator, then a secretary, and finally ended up with Gage.

"My name is John Milo," I told him. "I'm a friend of Big Joe Larson. He gave me your name when I told him I might have a job for someone like you."

"Fine. Why don't you come over to the office?"

"I have reasons why I don't think it would be the smartest thing. There is a possibility that I might be followed, and I would rather they didn't know of any connection between us."

"Cops or hoods?"

"Hoods."

"Where are you staying?"

"The Cactus Palace."

"Then that's the answer," he said. "They have a fine bar and grill, and I'm often there for lunch. My habit is to go sit at the bar for a while before I move to a table. Let us say I'll be there within an hour. It shouldn't be too crowded. Come and sit next to me."

"How will I know you?"

He chuckled. "I weigh about three hundred pounds, Mr. Milo, so it should be easy to spot me."

"I'll see you then," I said. I hung up.

It was time for the second move. I went downstairs and got plenty of change. Then I found a public phone booth and put in a call to Washington, D.C. I was going to enjoy this call.

It took a little time, talking to several people and even using a code name, but I finally heard a gruff voice which I had often heard during the past several years. He was an Army general who had long worked for a government agency.

"Hello, General," I said.

"Milo," he said angrily. "Why are you calling me? You're not on duty."

"In a way I am. In a way I think I'm doing you a favor, but I'm also asking for a favor, which I think you owe me."

"What do you mean?"

"Recently," I said gently, "you were asked to do a favor for Intercontinental Insurance—a company in which you own stock and for which you hope to go to work when you retire."

"What are you insinuating, March?"

"I'm not insinuating anything, sir. I'm stating a fact. The company in question was anxious to put pressure on an employee who was on vacation in Hong Kong so that he would give up his vacation to do some work for them. They requested you to apply that pressure under the excuse that the case in question was important to the government—as well as to the company."

"What's the point of all this?" he asked harshly.

"I thought you might like to follow through with your efforts to be a good citizen. Do you recall the case in question, General?"

He cleared his throat. "I believe it involved the interstate theft of medical drugs and business machines and the possible international sale of these objects to what I consider an enemy country."

"Do you have a pencil handy, General?"

"Yes."

I gave him the number of the plane I had seen being loaded earlier. "That is the number of a freight plane owned by the Naples Air Express of Phoenix, Arizona. It took off with a full load sometime within the past hour. Its destination is Hong Kong or some airport very near there. Its cargo is destined for Red China. The cargo is also, I am certain, stolen property. I don't know what agency would be most interested in this, but I should think at least one would be."

"Yes, yes, I think you're right. You're sure about this, Milo?"

"Quite sure."

"Well," he said, suddenly sounding jovial, "this is very good of you, Milo. I shall see that it is entered on your record."

"Just a minute," I said. "I haven't finished yet. Now we come to some things you can do for me, and one more thing I can do for you—or some other government branch."

"What?" He didn't sound so jovial this time.

"Under the name of John Milo, with false papers, I recently smuggled some jade into this country. This was not stolen jade, and I did it in order to get certain information which you will find of great value. I no longer have the jade, but I do have photographs of it, as well as an appraisal of its value—all notarized. I am prepared to pay the proper duties on it, but I want if done quietly and with no charges."

"But—but ..."

"Remember your blood pressure, General. Under the same name of John Milo, I was recently arrested in Los Angeles and charged with five counts of felony, all involving stolen business machines. Since they took my fingerprints, it's only a matter of time before they find that John Milo is really Milo March, sometimes the pride of a certain secret agency. I want to be certain that those charges are dropped."

"But ..."

"Wait, General. In the case where I was arrested, there was an FBI man named Frank Newton. I think he was probably fairly intelligent, and I want to meet him in Los Angeles as soon as possible. But it must be secretly so that I am not spotted going to see him. This is my second favor to you."

"Milo, do you know what you're asking?" he demanded.

"Sure. I also know what I'm giving. Talk to some of your friends and see what they think."

"Where can you be reached?"

"I'm in Arizona at the moment, but I expect to go back to Los Angeles this afternoon. For at least two days I'll be at the Native Son Motel on Hollywood Boulevard. After that I don't know where I'll be, so I suggest a certain speed. It might even be embarrassing to you otherwise."

"Milo," he said, and he sounded as if he were choking, "one of these days you are going to go too far. If you don't end up in a civilian jail, you're going to find yourself back in the Army, and I'm personally going to see that you're court-martialed." He hung up without waiting for an answer from me.

TWELVE

I was laughing to myself as I left the phone booth. I knew that the General was on the verge of a stroke, but I also knew that he would work on all my requests. I had known him for a long time, since the days when he was a chicken colonel.* We fought every time we talked to each other, but there was also a lot of mutual respect.

There was still some time left before meeting Gage when I got back to my room. I poured a small shot of V.O. and relaxed while I waited. Finally I figured it was time for Gage to have arrived, so I went downstairs to the bar and grill. There was no chance of making a mistake about him. He was sitting at the bar by himself. He was so big he should have been using two stools. I went over and sat next to him without looking at him. I ordered a martini and waited until it had been served.

"You must be Henry Gage," I said.

"Everybody in Phoenix knows Henry Gage," he said. "Who are you?"

"John Milo."

"Got any ID?"

I pulled out the phony ones and showed them to him.

---

* Back in World War II, Sam Roberts and Milo had been in the OSS together. They spent eighteen months together behind the Nazi lines in Europe. Sam had been a colonel then. In *No Grave for March* (1953), he had two stars. By *The Splintered Man* (1955), he'd added a third.

"Now, how about you?" I asked. "Everyone in Phoenix may know you, but I'm not a native here."

He chuckled and pulled out his wallet. He showed me his license as a private detective. "The place is clean at the moment," he said. "Nothing but solid businessmen who won't think anything of the fact that we're talking. If anyone of a different stripe comes in, I'll let you know."

"Fair enough. You got time to do a job?"

"Always got time to do a job. You want a fast one or a slow one?"

"Fast. I need a report within two or three days. I don't need it so fine that we can count the hairs, but I do need good general information."

"Three hundred dollars a day and expenses."

"All right. Now, excuse me for a minute." I got up and went to the men's room. When I came back I had $1,500 folded up. I sat down and passed it to him. "There's fifteen hundred there. You can send the receipt to me in care of Joe Larson in Los Angeles. You can send the report the same way. Speed is important. If you can do it in one day, you can still keep all the money. If you need more money, call Joe and I'll wire it to you."

"What's the job?"

"First, you know a little guy about five feet six, a hundred and forty pounds, a face like a tanned weasel's, who dresses and looks like a hood?"

"Sounds like Billy Stetson."

"What does he do?"

"That's hard to say," he answered. "Offhand he doesn't

seem to do much—except that he travels quite a bit and he's very chummy with some men around here who claim to be retired but used to be big men in Las Vegas, Chicago, and New York. Maybe they still are."

"It fits," I said. "You know anything about the Naples Air Express here in Phoenix?"

For the first time he looked directly at me. "Boy, you don't fool around with anything small, do you?"

"Then you do know something about them?"

"I don't exactly know anything, but I can do a lot of guessing. As far as anybody knows, they deal in legitimate freight. They even do some local business, but not enough for the size of their equipment. It is generally believed that they do freighting nationally and to the East and Near East."

"Well, I want to know about them."

"In two or three days—or less?"

"I don't mean everything. I'd like to know something about the volume of their business, and some idea of where most of their freight comes from and how it gets here. If you can find out what the freight is, that's even better. Then I'd like to know who are the officers of the company, who runs it, and who works for it. The latter includes the pilots and even the freight handlers—and if the employees are local people or come from somewhere else. In the latter case, if possible, from where."

"That's it?" he asked.

"That's about it. Of course, I'd like to know a lot more, but if I have that, I might be able to get the rest. There's not enough time for you to dig after more—and it might be dangerous."

He sighed heavily. "Well, at least you've got a sense of humor. Okay, I'll get what I can for you and send it off to Joe. I imagine you want it sent special delivery?"

"That would help."

He looked at me curiously. "I don't even want to know why you want this information. But if you're playing around in that league, how come no hardware?"

I smiled. "I've got it, but I don't have a license for Arizona and I had no time to get one. I'll buckle it on when I cross back over the California border. I'll wait to hear from you."

He nodded and I got up and went over to a booth. The place was beginning to fill up and I wanted to be alone. I ordered another martini and some lunch. While I was eating, I became glad I had moved to the booth. A guy came in who looked like a larger twin of the one who had called on me earlier. He was careful not to look at me while he sat at the bar and nursed a bottle of beer.

I paid my check and went back into the hotel. The desk clerk looked up as I went by. "Oh, Mr. Milo," he said. "Someone called for you but didn't leave any message. I told him you were in the grill."

"How did you know that?" I asked.

"I noticed you going in, sir. I hope you got the call."

"Well, I think I got the message at least," I said.

I went on upstairs and put my things together. Then I phoned for a boy to come for my luggage and went down and checked out. As I got into my car, I noticed that the beer drinker was standing not far away, chewing on a toothpick.

I also noticed that as I drove away a car fell in behind me. It stayed with me until I hit the highway heading for California, then it disappeared. It was nice to know that somebody cared.

It was a boring trip back to Los Angeles, but I finally made it by late afternoon. By this time I was plenty tired. I had been up since daylight and had driven to Phoenix and back. I stopped before I reached the motel and picked up a fresh bottle of V.O. Then I went on to my room. I got some ice from the machine outside, made myself a stiff drink, and stripped off my clothes. I stretched out on the bed and enjoyed the drink. I enjoyed the second one, too, but fell asleep as soon as I'd finished it.

I was awakened by the phone. I groped for it and answered.

"John Milo?" a voice asked.

"Yes."

"Angelo wants you to call him." He hung up.

I looked out the window. It was just getting dark. I got dressed and went out to a public phone booth on the street. I put in the person-to-person call.

"Where are you calling from?" he asked when he came on.

"Where the hell do you think I'm calling from?" I snapped. "It's a public booth in Los Angeles, California. I was asleep when your messenger boy phoned."

He laughed. "Too much sleep will spoil your reflexes. I just wanted to tell you that you did a good job on the delivery. It was somebody else's fault that they thought you were late. There'll be somebody around tomorrow between eleven and twelve with something for you. It'll include enough to cover your expenses. And stay holed up where you are until you hear from me. It'll be a couple of days or so." He hung up.

I was getting tired of people hanging up on me.

I went back to the motel room. I took a shower and shaved and made myself a drink. Then I called Joe at the usual place.

"I'm back," I said when he came on the phone. "If you have to get in touch with me, I'm at the same motel as before. I saw your friend today and he's supposed to send a report in care of you. Otherwise, I think I'd better stay away from you. I'm liable to get a little hot before too long."

"I get you," he said. "I'll call you as soon as I get anything."

This time I had the satisfaction of hanging up. I finished my drink and went out.

I drove up to La Brea and then across it until I saw what looked like a nice restaurant. I parked and went in. I had a few martinis and then dinner, but decided I was getting damned tired of eating alone. I did a little pub crawling, getting myself mildly swacked, and so I went back to the motel where I watched television until I fell asleep.

I went out for breakfast the next morning, stopping at a store to buy some large manila envelopes, then headed back to the motel to wait for my mysterious visitor.

At about ten o'clock my phone rang. I picked it up and said hello.

"John Milo?" a voice asked. It sounded familiar.

"Yes."

"This is Frank."

It took me a second before I realized it was the FBI man. "Hello, Frank," I said.

"Are you free for lunch?" he asked.

"I could be. It depends on the guests and the spot."

"Just you and me. There's a place in Pasadena called the Sea Cove. I could meet you there at one o'clock."

"Okay. I'll be there."

I went back to waiting and sipping V.O. Then I thought I'd get smart. I phoned the car rental place I'd used before and asked them to bring me a Cadillac. They promised to have it at the motel shortly after twelve.

It was a few minutes past eleven when there was a knock on my door. I opened it and there stood another movie-type thug.

"John Milo?" he asked.

"Yes," I said, but I was getting tired of the question.

"I got something for you," he said. He pulled an envelope from his pocket and held it out.

"Thanks," I said. I took it by one corner and started to close the door.

"Don't you want to check it?" he asked.

"No," I said. "I don't think I'd get short-changed and I don't think you'd have guts enough to dip into it. Thanks for bringing it." This time I did shut the door.

A few minutes later I went outside and up to the corner to buy a newspaper and some cigarettes. I didn't see anyone watching me, but that didn't mean there wasn't someone. I went back to the motel.

About five minutes after twelve a man arrived with the Cadillac. I signed the papers, gave him the deposit, and ushered him out. I stood outside and watched him get into a small car that had been towed behind the Cadillac. Nobody stopped him for any idle conversation.

I went back into the room and picked up the phone. I told

the office that I was going out to have lunch in the neighbor-hood and if anyone called to tell them I wouldn't be gone long. Then I got into the Cadillac and drove off.

I checked carefully, but there didn't seem to be anyone following me. If anyone had been watching the motel, the Cadillac might have thrown them off, since they'd be watching for the Ford I'd rented in Burbank.

I found the Sea Cove with a minimum of trouble. When I went in I spotted Frank at once, sitting at a table in a dark corner of the restaurant. But I didn't head for his table until I had looked at the other people there. I didn't recognize anyone—not that it meant too much. The organization probably had hundreds of men I didn't know. But I finally went over to the table anyway.

"Careful, aren't you?" he said with a smile as I sat down.

"I like staying alive," I said. "It's a habit I got into years ago and I haven't been able to break it. You know, that was a pretty corny act you put on in the police station when you were yelling for your lawyer."

He smiled. "I guess it was. Now, who the hell are you?"

A waitress was approaching us with a tray and two drinks on it. "I remembered," he said, "that you liked martinis and I took the liberty of ordering one for you in advance."

She put the drinks down and left. I took a sip and then looked at him.

"You mean you haven't received a report on my finger-prints yet?"

"Sure, I have," he said. He sounded disgusted. "A lot of good that did. It said that the prints belonged to a man named

Milo March. The report indicated only two things about this Milo March. He was an officer in the United States Army and is still an officer in the Reserves. It also indicated he had a high security clearance. It didn't say anything about him running around with phony papers. When the Washington office tried to get more information, it ran into a blank wall. We're not accustomed to that."

"Frustrating, isn't it?" I said, smiling.

"Then I get orders to contact you at that motel and arrange a quiet meeting. So—who the hell are you?"

"Just a guy named Milo March. Tell me something now. When you pulled that little business on Alameda Street, were you working on such matters as business machines and medical drugs, or were you working on something else and stumbled into that?"

"Machines and drugs," he said reluctantly.

"Then what were you doing Mickey Mousing around with booze?"

"I thought it might lead to something else—which it did. What were you doing fooling around with liquor?"

"The same thing. And it led to the same place. You haven't had much luck yet with the machines and drugs, have you?"

"We did arrest a few people the other day, if you remember."

"Pretty much small fry and at least one innocent person."

"We also have complete information on a shipment of the stolen merchandise out of this country, and it has probably already been seized by this time."

"Where'd you hear that? From Washington?"

"As a matter of fact, yes."

"They might have been considerate enough," I said, "to have told you that all of the information on that shipment came from me yesterday afternoon just about the time the plane took off—by phone from Arizona."

He looked startled. "To the Bureau?"

"No. To a man who is very important in another government agency and who obviously passed the information along to you and others."

"We also," he said, "have information that an American national is under arrest in Hong Kong, charged with possession of certain stolen medical drugs from this country."

I smiled. "I didn't telephone that to Washington, but that man—named Manny Keller—is under arrest because of me. I was in Hong Kong at the time. If you got a complete report, you will know that Manny Keller and his companion, Bernie Henderson, were hijacked by five Chinese who were chased off by a Caucasian. That was me. They were chased off while Manny Keller still had some drugs in his possession. The Hong Kong police did not just happen to be nearby. They had been told to be."

"Why?" he asked.

"It's not why I have a high security rating nor why you had trouble getting information about me, but I am an insurance investigator, and I work for the company that insured almost everything involved. I was on vacation, and they asked me to interrupt it and try to solve the case. When they sent me a file, it contained nothing. I had to start from nothing. I started with Manny Keller."

"Where has it taken you?"

"Quite a distance. I have some proof and I expect to have some more. You are welcome to all of it. I am not interested in any credit. I'm interested in stopping what is going on. Not only the stealing, but the dealing with Red China. Now, do you want me to cooperate with you or not?"

He smiled for the first time. "I don't have much choice. I've had my orders. What do you have?"

"Several things, and I expect more today or tomorrow." I motioned to the waitress and waited until we had two more drinks. Then I put one of my manila envelopes on the table, but held on to it. "I have to tell you that I have already worked my way, under the name of John Milo, into taking Manny Keller's place."

"Working for whom?"

"You mean you don't know? The Syndicate. You will learn the identity of the specific man shortly. They have been operating in two ways. The drugs have gone from here to Hong Kong by courier. That was Manny Keller. I'm supposed to be the new courier. The business machines have gone by air freight through the Naples Air Express of Phoenix, Arizona. Because of Keller's arrest, it was decided to send the next drug shipment by the same plane. I made my first delivery of the drugs to Arizona yesterday. That is how I got the number of the plane."

He looked thoughtful. "We've had some interest in them before, but I don't think we have anything connecting them with this."

"Well, they are in up to their eyebrows. I was supposed to

be paid one thousand dollars plus expenses for that delivery. The money is supposed to be in a smaller envelope inside of this one. It was delivered to me this morning. I haven't touched it except at one corner. There should be at least the fingerprints of the man who delivered it. Possibly the money can be traced."

He took the manila envelope and glanced inside it. "We'll check it out. Thanks. What else do you have?"

"Did you ever hear of Angelo Bacci?"

He nodded. "He's an important man in the Syndicate."

"And a don in the Mafia," I said. I put another manila envelope on the table. "He is masterminding the job you're on. Here are some tape recordings between Bacci and a man named Larry Blake, who also works in Hong Kong. There is also a recording of a conversation in which he hired me to take Keller's place."

He looked a little more enthusiastic as he took that envelope.

"Today or tomorrow," I continued, "I will have some material for you on the airline in Phoenix. It won't solve everything for you, but it will give you a lot of leads you need. How can I get it to you quickly?"

"Department of Justice office addressed to me. Mark it special. The local office. What's in the other envelope?" I handed it to him without comment. He opened it and looked at the contents with a puzzled expression. "What's this?" he asked.

"Part of the price you—or someone in the government—have to pay for my cooperation."

"What does that mean?"

"I've been breaking a few laws," I said with a smile. "I've been operating as John Milo with forged papers. I've made one trip out of the country and back under that name. On my last trip back I returned with some jade. What you have there is an appraisal of the value of the jade, photographs of every piece, and a bill of sale to Angelo Bacci. The jade was smuggled into this country by me. I am, however, as I've already told my friend in Washington, prepared to pay the full amount of the duty. But quietly. No charges on any count—including the bust you and your friends gave me here."

"Good God," he exclaimed. "Do you know what you're telling me?"

"Sure. Do you know what I'm giving you?"

He shook his head. "That doesn't excuse breaking that many laws. Where did you get the forged papers?"

"From my fairy godmother," I said gently. "You may report all of this back to Washington. Since they love channels, I suggest that they follow back through the information about the plane and the order that you get in touch with me, and see what the reaction is."

He was still looking shocked. "But the law ..."

"Frank," I said gently, "I respect the laws as much as you do. I didn't break any laws carelessly. And I was taught by a government agency, as important as your own, to break the kind of laws I do."

"I don't like it," he said. "Was this jade stolen?"

"Yes and no. It was stolen in Red China and brought into

Hong Kong. I doubt, however, that there will be any charge of its being stolen. Therefore, it was bought legitimately."

"From whom?"

"A little Chinese on the street. He was selling Hong Kong postcards—very naughty—and jade. I bought some of both. Would you like to see the postcards?"

"Heaven forbid." He shuddered. "Well, I can't promise you anything. I'll send through a report."

"Do that. And I can't promise anything until we've reached what is laughingly called a gentlemen's agreement."

"Let's have lunch," he said wearily.

We ordered lunch. I ordered another drink with mine. He looked as if he needed one, but he passed it up. I waited until we had finished lunch and were having coffee before I said any more.

"There is one thing I would like to suggest," I said then.

"What?"

"I presume that you have certain electronic gadgets. Put one in a car and keep a constant tail on me starting today. I have a couple of transistor microphones, so you can pick up and record anything in which I participate. But make sure that you're prepared to follow me anywhere."

"Why?"

"I have an idea the heat is going to be on me soon. If I'm right, you might learn some things that will be valuable."

"All right," he said. "I'll arrange it as soon as I get back to the office."

"I have two cars," I said. "One is a Ford Galaxie and the other is a Cadillac. Both are rented." I gave him a slip of paper.

"Here are the license numbers of both cars. Tell your man to be prepared to go as far as Las Vegas."

He nodded and we finished our coffee. I picked up the check, despite his protest, and left first.

I got in the car and headed back to Los Angeles. I couldn't find any evidence, but I had a strange feeling that I was being followed.

When I reached the motel there was a message that Mr. Larson had called. As soon as I got into my room I called him back.

"Where are you?" he asked.

"In the motel."

"Stay there. I'll call you right back from a public booth."

I waited two or three minutes and the phone rang again. It was Joe. "I didn't want to talk from that phone," he said. "There was a guy around this afternoon. I know him from Las Vegas, but only slightly. He got into casual conversation with me, but all he wanted to talk about was you. Are you in trouble?"

"No, but I wouldn't be surprised if I'm getting a little warm around the edges."

"Need help?"

"No, thanks, Joe. I think it'll work out all right."

"Okay." He sounded disappointed. "Just remember I'm here."

"I will."

I hung up and took a nap. I figured I was going to need all the rest I could get. Later, I got up and went out. I was being followed, but carefully enough so that I figured it was the

FBI. There may have been another car back of him. I ignored the whole problem. I went to a good restaurant and had some cocktails and a good dinner. I stopped at a couple of bars afterwards, then went back to the motel. I watched television and drank until I was sleepy.

I was awakened the next morning by the phone. It was Joe Larson. "There's a special-delivery letter for you," he said.

"Can you get it to me here?" I asked. "I don't think you should bring it yourself."

"Sure. I'll send it by a broad. They won't think so much of that. Give her a few bucks."

I hung up and made myself a drink while I waited. It was about thirty minutes before there was a hesitant knock on the door. I opened it and a woman stood there. She had obviously seen better days, but she was still attractive.

"Mr. Milo?" she asked uncertainly. "Big Joe told me to come and see you."

"Come in, honey," I said.

She came into the room and handed me an envelope. I saw her looking at my drink, so I made one for her. I opened the envelope and looked at the report. It was pretty good. By the time I'd finished looking at it, she'd finished the drink. I took out fifty dollars and gave it to her. She stared at it and up at me again.

"Do you know what you gave me?" she asked.

"Sure. Go off and spend it. But don't tell anyone where you got it."

"I won't," she said fervently. She scurried from the room.

I put the report in a motel envelope and addressed it. Then

I called a delivery service and asked them to pick up an envelope at the office of the motel. I clipped a ten-dollar bill to the envelope and went to the office. I told them there would be someone from the delivery service coming around to pick it up, and the change from the ten dollars was to go to the boy. I then went out to get some breakfast, knowing that I would be followed and that there would be less chance of anyone noticing the delivery boy.

I stopped at The Tippler and had a couple of drinks and then had breakfast next door. After that I picked up a paper and went back to the motel.

The first phone call came in a little more than an hour. "This is Frank," he said. "It arrived. Thanks."

"Nothing to it," I said, "but I have a hunch you'd better get ready for action."

"Okay." He hung up.

The next call came about noon. This time it was one of those mysterious voices again. "John Milo?" he asked.

"Yes."

"Angelo wants to see you as soon as possible up north at home base."

"Okay," I said cheerfully, "tell him I'm on my way."

I then called the first rental place and told them to pick up the Ford Galaxie, and to take what I owed them out of the deposit and mail the rest of it to me at the Native Son. I left word with the desk that they were coming for the Ford and that I would be back. Then I took off in the Cadillac, headed for Las Vegas. I had two companions part of the way, then only one.

I made good time all the way to Las Vegas and pulled into

the Sultan's Palace. I left the Cadillac at the front entrance and went in and registered. I asked the clerk to tell Mr. Bacci that I was there and would be at the bar.

I wasn't there long before he showed up. He slipped onto the stool next to me. "How are you, John?" he asked.

"Fine," I said. "What's up?"

"We're having a little meeting," he said. "It involves things you'll be working on, so I wanted you to be here."

"When's the meeting?"

"Right away—now that you're here. Do you have a car?"

"Yes. I drove up from Los Angeles."

"Okay. Let's go. You can follow me to the meeting place."

We went out to the front of the hotel. Both our cars were waiting. I got into mine and waited for him to pull out. I then followed him closely. I was pleased to see that another car was following us.

We drove out beyond the city limits and finally came to a pleasant-looking little house set back from the road. The front yard was filled with colorful flowers. We pulled into the driveway and stopped.

"Nice, huh?" Angelo Bacci said as we got out of our cars. "Where else could we find such a nice place to meet?" He slapped me on the left shoulder, but I had the feeling that it was more to see if I was wearing my shoulder holster than as a friendly gesture.

I wasn't wearing it. I had removed it on the way up and tucked the gun under my belt in the back.

We walked up to the front of the house, and he opened the door. "Go on in, John," he said.

I stepped through the door. At the same time I turned on the microphone in my tie clasp. Bacci followed me in and closed the door. Then I saw we weren't alone. The tall blond guy who was known as Larry Blake was sitting in a chair across the room. He was holding a gun—pointed at me.

"Come right in, sucker," he said.

TWELVE AND ONE-HALF

It was pretty much what I had expected. But I was there, and I didn't know what I could do except follow the script they had written.

"I thought this was a friendly meeting," I said.

"It is, sucker," Larry Blake said. He looked beyond me. "Is he clean?"

"I think so," Bacci said from behind me, "but we'll make sure." He patted me beneath both arms and then patted my pockets. "Yeah, he's clean."

"Sit down, sucker," Blake said, motioning to the chair across from him.

I went over and sat down. I looked up at Bacci. "What the hell is all this?"

"We don't like double-crossers," Bacci said, "and we're going to teach you what happens to them. It may be the last thing you ever learn."

"What the hell's wrong with you?" I demanded.

"I'll tell you," he said softly. "First, as I mentioned to you before, you were right on the spot when Manny Keller was hijacked and then dumped in the laps of the cops. Well, you're allowed one accident like that. But day before yesterday you made a delivery of drugs for us to Phoenix, Arizona. Because there was a mix-up about the flight time, you were permitted to see the plane that was being loaded. Would you be surprised to learn that the ship was busted when it landed at the end of its trip, and everything on it was grabbed by the cops?"

"How did that happen?" I asked. I wasn't trying to win any Academy Award. I didn't think there was any point in wasting it on them.

"I'll give you one guess," Bacci said. "Now, let's move along to yesterday. You went to Pasadena and had a long lunch with a Federal agent. Strangely enough, he was the man working on the case when you were arrested along with some of our men."

I took out a cigarette and lit it. I settled into a more comfortable position in the chair in the meantime slipping my gun out onto the seat.

"What Federal agent?" I asked.

"You know damn well which one. I don't think you had enough to give him to hurt us too much, and that's why you're not going to get another chance."

"Goodness, you sound tough," I said. "What are you going to do? Shoot me?"

"That's the general idea, sucker," Larry Blake said.

"Then what's all the talk about?" I asked. At the same time I flipped my burning cigarette straight at Blake and dived out of the chair with the gun in my hand. I hit the floor rolling.

Blake's gun went off, sounding like a cannon in the room. But I'd thrown him off balance. At first I thought it had been completely successful, but then I realized there was a burning sensation in my left shoulder. I didn't have any time to see what was causing it. Larry Blake was bringing his gun around to bear on me again. I didn't waste any time being fancy. I shot him right in the middle. His white shirt began to turn red and there was a surprised look on his face as he tumbled to the floor.

I twisted around to look at Bacci. He was trying to get a gun out of his pocket.

"You," I said, "I'm going to save." I took careful aim and shot him through the knee. He screamed and went down, his gun skidding across the carpet.

There was the sound of pounding feet outside and I turned to face the door. It burst open and two men dashed in and skidded to a halt. I didn't know one of them, but the other was Frank Newton.

"Well," I said, "it was nice of you to come to the party, but why didn't you try to get here on time?" Frank came directly to me, putting his gun away. He started to look at my shoulder, so I decided I might as well look too. It was covered with blood. He pulled out a handkerchief and began to stuff it inside my shirt.

"Jack will take care of the other two," he said, "and I'll get you to the hospital right away. You did a good job, March."

I think I got a little faint then, because the next thing I remembered we were in my Cadillac and he was driving. I fished out a cigarette and lit it.

"What about our gentlemen's agreement?" I asked.

"There are no charges against you," he said gruffly. "You can pay the duties on the jade anytime it's convenient. Now shut up while I get you to a hospital."

"It's not that serious," I said. "And I have to do one thing before we go to the hospital."

"What?"

"Stop at a telegraph office."

"You're crazy. You can do that later."

"Stop at a telegraph office or I'll jump out of the car."

He said something under his breath, but he stopped when we came to a Western Union. He went in with me and flashed his identification when the clerk looked as if he would scream at the sight of my bloody shoulder. First I dictated a telegram to Martin Raymond. It read:

EVERYTHING UNDER CONTROL. WILL NOW FINISH MY VACATION. PLEASE HAVE CHECK READY FOR ME WHEN I RETURN TO WORK. GIVE MY LOVE TO THE BOARD OF DIRECTORS. I DON'T KNOW WHAT I'D DO WITHOUT THEM.

MILO

The next one was a cablegram that went to Mei Hsu in Hong Kong:

AM COMING BACK TO FINISH MY VACATION. BREAK OUT THE DRAGON DANCERS AND THE FIRECRACKERS.

LOVE, MILO

I paid for the messages and turned to the FBI agent. "Onward to the hospital, Frank Nightingale," I said, but my voice didn't sound as strong as it should have.

AFTERWORD

The Drinking Life

"An amazing man is Milo March, the insurance investigator who solves the most complicated crimes while imbibing an inordinate amount of alcohol, which at no time seems to slow down his thinking or his muscles."
—*Amarillo Globe-Times*

In a review of *The Flaming Man,* Steve Lewis writes in his *Mystery File* blog that "if you cut out the references to drinking, the book would be at least 20 pages shorter. Milo March is one of those guys who could really put it away. For breakfast, lunch, dinner, bedtime and every other half hour in between, another drink. From one bar to another, it seems, nonstop."

A more literary comment about the same book comes from mystery historian Mike Grost: "Whenever Milo March wants to interview a suspect, or track down a clue, he goes to another bar to do it. There is something surrealistic about this, as well as being a satire on the traditional private eye tale. It is consistent with Crossen's depiction of substance abuse throughout his fiction."

Did we even call it substance abuse in the 1960s and '70s? Ken Crossen may not have depicted substance abuse so much as his own attitude toward the drinking life. In *Death to the*

Brides, after returning from Vietnam, a trip that included a trek through the jungle with Viet Cong soldiers, Milo says, "The most exciting drink I had while I was gone was the blood of a freshly killed pig mixed with warm wine. It almost made me join Alcoholics Anonymous, but my sanity returned in time."

When other characters remark on Milo's drinking, this could be the author's way of creating an opportunity to defend his own view. Milo sometimes responds with humor:

FIRST TIME IN PAPERBACK

A MILO MARCH MYSTERY

2

M. E. CHABER
"Plenty of slam-bang action."
—N.Y. TIMES

A MAN IN THE MIDDLE

"Do you always drink that much?" she asked.

"No, sometimes I drink more."

And sometimes with reason:

"It's a medical fact that a man of my size can drink an ounce of liquor an hour and never feel it. So I will have had six ounces and a dinner in seven hours."

Mostly he is just matter-of-fact, as when a bullet wound sends him to the hospital and the doctor says:

"The lab tests came out fine. There was, however, one strange thing about the test of your blood. It showed a rather high content of alcohol. How do you account for that?"

"By taking a drink when I feel like it."

In several books we see Milo pacing his drinks or eating strategically, including downing a rare steak and a glass of milk. In *So Dead the Rose,* he gets stoned in the process of plying a Soviet official with vodka so as to steal his Zis limo. Milo sobers up enough to drive the escape vehicle by munching hunks of black bread and cheese.

Drinking serves many purposes for Milo, and he acknowledges that it often provides liquid courage or acts as a tranquilizer. He hates air travel, which he claims is boring (he doesn't admit it's scary), and no matter the time of day, he always asks the stewardess for several mini-bottles so he can fall asleep until the flight lands.

Will Murray, in a surprisingly judgmental passage in *Twentieth-Century Crime and Mystery Writers* (1980), writes that "March is a hedonist, albeit a tough hedonist, who dislikes legwork or violence and prefers large expense accounts, fine restaurants, good drink, and at least two women per novel. He spends a great deal of each novel indulging himself, while his presence actuates violent events among his quarry." But that is precisely Milo's method: "I don't go around looking for clues. I just sit around, sometimes drinking as much brandy as I can, and let things drift in my direction. Whatever comes to me, I investigate."

A writer or artist sometimes appears to be doing nothing

but may actually be immersed in the creative process. Similarly, Milo's skull work doesn't show: "I had a cup of coffee, then a drink, and finally stretched out on the bed. I thought about the case and fell asleep." The method is both intuitive and practical: "Many people complain that I drink a lot. I do, but I also do the things that have to be done."

Among Ken Crossen's papers I was amused to find this comment by his foreign rights agent in London, Elaine Greene, who wrote to him on December 31, 1968, about a *Publisher's Weekly* review that noted Milo's over-beveraged condition: "I thought the PW remark about drinking was exaggerated, but contained a grain of truth. It's not the quantity but the loving detail that gets a bit overdone. Couldn't you now and then rush a bit more quickly past the mixing and skip a bit of the picking up and putting down of glasses? Sorry to seem to side with the enemy but if you look at the first three pages of A MAN IN THE MIDDLE with a cold eye, I think you might even agree."

For the record: The hardcover first edition of *A Man in the Middle* (1967) contains three drinks in the first three pages: one a martini at poolside during his vacation, and two drinks (one of them "small") poured from a bottle of V.O. in his hotel room. He does pick them up and put them down a couple of times, but I think other books in the series make much more of the clinking of ice cubes, toasts, and other ritual activities. I read the entire series twice, one book after the other, and sometimes felt the drinking details were overdone, but then booze was also entirely forgotten during many pages filled with action.

ELAINE GREENE LTD.
LITERARY AGENCY

DIRECTORS
ELAINE GREENE (U.S.A.)
PETER JANSON-SMITH

42 GREAT RUSSELL STREET,
LONDON, W.C.1.
Telephone: 01-580 8055
Cables: JASMITH LONDON W.C.1.

Kendell Foster Crossen Esq
Apt. 5
503 Mill Street
Reno, Nevada
U.S.A.

31 December 1968

Dear Ken,

There's no hope on earth of getting a quick cheque from any Dutch
publisher, they're the slowest payers on earth. I will, though,
take the risk that they'll pay in the end. I think it's easiest
to deduct commissions first, and then pay AFA when the money comes
in. (I send them commission only on a lot of their clients who
for various reasons do not want their money in America.) The total
commission is 19% -- 7% to the Dutch agent, 6% each to AFA and me.
I am therefore asking our Accounts Department to apply for a dollar
draft for $162 in your favour. It is, alas, not as simple as send-
ing you a cheque, because currency restrictions remain with us and
we need Bank of England approval for every single transfer. I'm
only sorry that things are so rough for you.

I thought the PW remark about drinking was exaggerated, but contained a grain of truth. It's not the quantity but the loving detail
that gets a bit overdone. Couldn't you now and then rush a bit more
quickly past the mixing and skip a bit of the picking up and putting
down of glasses? Sorry to seem to side with the enemy but if you
look at the first three pages of A MAN IN THE MIDDLE with a cold
eye, I think you might even agree.

I'm glad you're liking Reno, and above all that you are feeling so much
better. I look forward to getting copies of both books and I'll do
my damnedest to sell them for you.

I hope 1969 will be full of good health and happiness and success.

Yours ever,

Elaine

"Some job. All you do is sleep, hang around with broads,
and drink booze. And you get paid for it." That is how one

character describes Milo March. He does all of those things, of course. But those aren't the only things he does. For example, in *The Gallows Garden* he recites a medieval Spanish poem in praise of short women. As Milo attests elsewhere with a tinge of irony: "Occasionally, between drinks, I read a book."

ABOUT THE AUTHOR

Kendell Foster Crossen
(1910–1981), the only child
of Samuel Richard Cros-
sen and Clo Foster Cros-
sen, was born on a farm
outside Albany in Athens
County, Ohio—a village of
some 550 souls in the year
of this birth. His ancestors
on his mother's side include
the 19th-century songwriter
Stephen Collins Foster
("Oh! Susanna"); William

Allen, founder of Allentown, Pennsylvania; and Ebenezer
Foster, one of the Minute Men who sprang to arms at the
Lexington alarm in April 1775.

Ken went to Rio Grande College on a football scholarship
but stayed only one year. "When I was fairly young, I devel-
oped the disgusting habit of reading," says Milo March,
and it seems Ken Crossen, too, preferred self-education.
He loved literature and poetry; favorite authors included
Christopher Marlowe and Robert Service. He also enjoyed
participant sports and was a semi-pro fighter in the heavy-

weight class. He became a practicing magician and had a passion for chess.

After college Ken wrote several one-act plays that were produced in a small Cleveland theater. He worked in steel mills and Fisher Body plants. Then he was employed as an insurance investigator, or "claims adjuster," in Cleveland. But he left the job and returned to the theater, now as a performer: a tumbling clown in the Tom Mix Circus; a comic and carnival barker for a tent show, and an actor in a medicine show.

In 1935, Ken hitchhiked to New York City with a typewriter under his arm, and found work with the WPA Writers' Project, covering cricket for the *New York City Guidebook*. In 1936, he was hired by the Munsey Publishing Company as associate editor of the popular *Detective Fiction Weekly*. The company asked him to come up with a character to compete with The Shadow, and thus was born a unique superhero of pulps, comic books, and radio—The Green Lama, an American mystic trained in Tibetan Buddhism.

Crossen sold his first story, "The Aaron Burr Murder Case," to *Detective Fiction Weekly* in September 1939, but says he didn't begin to make a living from writing till 1941. He tried his hand at publishing true crime magazines, comics, and a picture magazine, without great success, so he set out for Hollywood. From his typewriter flowed hundreds of stories, short novels for magazines, scripts radio, television, and film, nonfiction articles. He delved into science fiction in the 1950s, starting with "Restricted Clientele" (February 1951). His dystopian novels *Year of Consent* and *The Rest Must Die* also appeared in this decade.

In the course of his career Ken Crossen acquired six pseud-
onyms: Richard Foster, Bennett Barlay, Kent Richards, Clay
Richards, Christopher Monig, and M.E. Chaber. The variety
was necessary because different publishers wanted to reserve
specific bylines for their own publications. Ken based "M.E.
Chaber" on the Hebrew word for "author," *mechaber.*

In the early '50s, as M.E. Chaber, Crossen began to write
a series of full-length mystery/espionage novels featuring
Milo March, an insurance investigator. The first, *Hangman's
Harvest,* was published in 1952. In all, there are twenty-two
Milo March novels. One, *The Man Inside,* was made into a
British film starring Jack Palance.

Most of Ken's characters were private detectives, and Milo
was the most popular. Paperback Library reissued twenty-five
Crossen titles in 1970–1971, with covers by Robert McGinnis. Twenty were Milo March novels, four featured an insurance investigator named Brian Brett, and one was about CIA
agent Kim Locke.

Crossen excelled at producing well-plotted entertainment
with fast-moving action. His research skills were a strong
asset, back when research meant long hours searching library
microfilms and poring over street maps and hotel floorplans.
His imagination took him to many international hot spots,
although he himself never traveled abroad. Like Milo March,
he hated flying ("When you've seen one cloud, you've seen
them all").

Ken Crossen was married four times. With his first wife he
had three children (Stephen, Karen, Kendra) and with his
second a son (David). He lived in New York, Florida, South-

ern California, Nevada, and other parts of the country. Milo March moves from Denver to New York City after five books of the series, with an apartment on Perry Street in Greenwich Village; that's where Ken lived, too. His and Milo's favorite watering hole was the Blue Mill Tavern, a short walk from the apartment.

Ken Crossen was a combination of many of the traits of his different male characters: tough, adventuresome, with a taste for gin and shapely women. But perhaps the best observation was made in an obituary written by sci-fi writer Avram Davidson, who described Ken as a fundamentally gentle person who had been buffeted by many winds.